INTERMENT

A Novel by

Terry Cassidy

To Mary Joy

Terry Cassidy

CHAPTER 1

Parksville, British Columbia, June, 1994

I saw the newspaper story in a copy of a Toronto tabloid that Ken had brought on his last trip. I think he grabbed it to wrap around a decanter he gave me on my birthday. Anyway, the day after he left, I found the paper in the top drawer of the guest room dresser.

Since Dee died three years ago, I don't have too many visitors. Ken, of course, when he can get away, Laura and her husband, Vic, about once a year. No grandchildren yet, and I find myself resenting that, in a way. Stupid. My Dad saw very little of Laura and Ken, but I don't know if their presence would have healed the scar tissue of our relationship. Maybe it would have — grandparents are supposed to have an unconditional set of ties with grandchildren, and perhaps if I had seen him more with Laura and Ken, I would have been able to see through the pitted and battered armour my father wore right up to his illness.

The story: it was simple enough. Gloria Peet, described as a "colourful carnival worker, showgirl and a few other things" by the flip writer of the piece, had died in her one-bedroom apartment a few days before — I glanced at the date of the paper, Saturday, May 28 — so the Tuesday mentioned in the story must have been May 24. Evidently, Gloria had worked under many names in the past, some of which had earned her notoriety; for example, as Gennifer Passion, she had been the mistress of a well-known Toronto city councillor in the mid sixties. The man (now dead) would have been mortified to know that "Gennifer" was pushing fifty. As the reporter put it, her faith in preservatives was strong and well justified. Three more aliases were listed, all with the initials "G.P."

"Either Miss Peet had some expensive monogrammed luggage, or she was helping her memory along. She never sank to 'General Purpose', but recovered her birth name when she applied for her Old Age Security and found that the government wanted proof of identity."

"Miss Peet came from Cobalt, a boom mining town in Northern Ontario, where she was born in 1918. She left after the boom burst, but never forgot her roots. On her bedside table was a piece of ore, a rock with what looked like a massive cable imbedded in it. A friend said that Gloria called it 'wire silver', a piece of high-grade (ie, stolen) silver that her father had given her a year before he was killed in an underground accident."

I already knew that Gloria Peet had come from Cobalt. The surprising thing was that she died last month in Toronto, because I had found her body in 1949, almost half a century ago.

I took the paper out to the deck, and sat looking at Georgia Strait and the hint of darkness on the horizon that was the mainland. I've flown east so many times that it is no effort of the imagination to think of the mountains, ridge after ridge, passing below, then the slough-dotted prairies, and then the Shield, but now my imagination takes me lower, to the ten thousand feet disdained by jets, so that I can see the scarred, raked rock of the land and the water covering half of it, seeping into the great rivers that flow northeast into Hudson Bay.

Imagination has a rougher task taking me back to that summer when I was thirteen. When someone was thirteen, because "I", the me sitting here on this deck, am made up of that person plus all the persons I have been in the years between then and now, one person sliding into another like those Russian dolls that look identical except for size. I wonder why the artists don't age those dolls from the inside out. The child is father to the man, no, the child is kernel to the man, and natural piety should be reserved to real fathers. Did my father want piety from me? What did I owe him, and how could I know it? Maybe if I were to look at my thirteen year old self as another person, call him Jimmy, and say "He said…" and "he woke up" to that faraway summer, that hot, hot summer of 1949 …

The day was going to be hot, he could feel that. He stretched and looked down at the tent his splayed feet made of the sheet. It looked like a marquee army tent, except for the colour. He'd asked Dad if he and the other cadets would be sleeping in tents like that at Ipperwash. The name was different, not English, not Indian or French. Dad didn't know where the name came from, though he'd been in the army all those years with the Algonquins, over in England, then France, Holland and Germany, and came back a hero, with the Military Medal.

His feet waggled, and the tent swayed violently as if in a sudden storm. It was almost six, maybe five to. He'd never had a watch, and there was only the one clock in the house, on the kitchen wall, but he didn't really need one. He felt the rhythm of the day without thinking, and always knew what time it was, within ten minutes or so. The French Church would ring the Angelus at around six, exactly three minutes before St. Patrick's. The noon siren, the "official" time of Cobalt came right after the noon French Angelus, and about ten seconds before the start of St. Patrick's bell. (Father Delaney told the altar boy on duty to wait for the siren). Now he heard the French Angelus begin, way over on Lang Street, the bell hardly heard up here on Nickel Street. In the silences, he heard a "tap-tap-tap" that was his mother stirring the oatmeal. He waited. St. Patrick's was just down where the highway turned sharply after entering the town, only about half a mile from his house. Now it started, and he mumbled the prayers. It was OK to stay lying down for these prayers, not like night time, because the Angelus was one of those things that caught you in the middle of whatever you were doing, and you were supposed to just pause for the prayer, not make a show of it.

Besides, he didn't have to get up at all. First day of exams, and he was exempted. This was the payoff, the thing that made up for some of the teasing he took for getting good marks. Not that he studied much, just that school was really easy for him, and always had been. Two years before, Miss Kelly asked Dad if it might be best for him to write the High School Entrance exams. Nobody asked him. It was the end of May, and he had to do all the Grade Eight work in less than a month. Of course, he'd been sitting in the Grade Seven rows, right between the Grade Sixes and the Grade Eights, all year, and couldn't help overhearing everything the Grade Eights did. Anyway, he'd started high school at age eleven, and not big for his age either. Not an easy life, but he'd been the policeman's son ever since Dad came back from the war, and he'd developed some ability to take it. His mouth was his protection, and some guys, who could take him apart if they wanted to, let him be a sort of mascot because he could out-talk them.

So now he could stay in bed if he wanted to. Maybe till eight, when his mother, on the basis that it was a beautiful day, would roust him out of bed, and the oatmeal would be cold. He got up suddenly, and jumped from the top bunk, landing lightly. He wouldn't even have to deliver the *Nugget* today, because Charlie was doing it on Mondays, getting familiar so he could take over the route for the summer. Willy was already downstairs, a ferocious seven-year old appetite drawing him to the kitchen every morning before breakfast was ready. Jimmy hung his pyjamas in the closet and dressed quickly, underwear, shorts, shirt and runners. Then he grabbed his swimsuit.

Mom sat down with her coffee as he finished his porridge. "And how are you going to use the first day of your summer?"

"Oh, I guess I'll go see Harry. We might take a hike. Can I make a sandwich?"

"Sure. There's chokecherry jelly in the fridge, and you know where the peanut butter is." Jimmy put his bowl in the sink. Mom would normally save the dishes till lunch, but these hot days, she liked to let the fire go out in the big stove, and the hot water tank on the side would cool down. So she'd probably do them earlier. He cut two pieces of bread from the high loaf — Mom's theory was that if you were going to bake bread, it might as well be BIG bread — and started making his sandwich.

"Where do you think you'll go?" Normally, she wasn't that curious about kid plans, and he looked at her sharply, but it was just friendly interest on her part. Maybe she felt a little envious of his freedom?

"Maybe we'll walk the pipeline over to the ranger station." Even within town the pipelines were routes for kids, smoother than many of the sidewalks, sometimes just a few feet from the ground up to about twelve feet. A web of them covered the town, stretching out to outlying minesites. The main ones still carried compressed air to power the mines still operating. Jimmy often went down to the ranger tower on the main line, about 36 inches diameter, which went all the way to Hound Chutes, the compressing station on the Montreal River. Today, the cast iron pipe would get very hot, but you could pause at the joints, where enough air came past the gaskets to form frost, and you could cool your shoes.

She got up and poured herself another cup of coffee. "Have a good time. We're glad you didn't have to write exams, you know." Her eyes strayed to her book lying beside her place at the kitchen table, and he knew he could go, that she wasn't really worried or envious. He remembered one time, during the war, when he'd come home from school to the old house over in the Wright Subdivision — he must have been in Grade Four — and she wasn't home. She came home ten minutes later, but for him it had been a miserable ten minutes. It turned out she had just been down the street with the baby, but Jimmy had never been prepared for a world in which his Mom would not be home when he got there.

Maybe Harry and he would go for a hike. Harry was the second youngest guy in Grade Ten (or Second Form, as some of the teachers called it), six months older than Jimmy, and pretty smart. He and Jimmy traded first place in every subject but French, where they both trailed well behind the guys from Lang Street, who spoke French at home. It must have been strange for them, like taking a Grade Two Reader when you're fifteen or sixteen. Anyway, Harry was exempted too, and they might as well do something together. Not right away. First the Sinkhole.

Instead of the stairs going down the hill towards the public school, he took the road that joined the highway near the old head frame, then through the smelter ruins down to the trickle of water that joined Cobalt Lake to Cross Lake. Not that Cobalt Lake was much of a lake any more — forty years of mine tailings had turned it into an opaque grey puddle. Some of these cyanide slime tailings penetrated up the creek, but generally the water here was simply muddy. Close to Cross Lake, the creek widened where an old mineshaft had filled with brown water, the Sinkhole, where all the kids swam. Nobody was here this morning, for the heat of the day hadn't really gotten going, and, besides, the grade school kids were getting ready to go to school, and most of the high school kids were getting ready for their first exam. Jimmy swiftly tore off his clothes and got into his swimsuit. Then he went back up the trail and found a fair sized rock, maybe twenty pounds, heavy enough.

Back at the edge of the water, he began his count. He would jump on twenty, no, fifty. 46, 47, 48, 49 ,,, 50. He was almost surprised to find himself in the water, plunging fast, pulled down by the rock. So fast, he got scared and dropped it, then twisted under water. No, he couldn't see anything. He kicked for the surface, and burst through it, sputtering. Maybe he'd turned in his jump, or maybe there wasn't enough light. The only guys who had done the stunt did it in the afternoons, when the sun was higher, and over to the west.

They would line up with their rocks, some of them just showoffs, like Gil and Pat. Then one would jump, and just disappear for ten minutes, to reappear just when the watchers were getting really scared. The trick was that there was a tunnel, an old sub-drift that went straight back under the spot they'd jumped from, and, about fifteen feet in, widened into a chamber that got air from the surface somehow. The daredevils — and Jimmy certainly wanted to be one — had to keep a sense of direction and sufficient breath to back their choice of where to swim in order to get back out to the Sinkhole. He longed to match the trick, but he knew himself well enough that he would have to do it in private before he did it before a crowd. Not today, he thought. He faced an additional hazard, because his Dad seemed to know through his pores exactly what happened anywhere in town, and who was involved. If he ever found out that Jimmy was attempting the Sinkhole Disappearing Act, his anger would be towering.

Dad was known though Cobalt either as "Mr. Thorpe, sir" (by everyone under twenty) or "Lil" (everyone else). The "Lil" was a contraction of "Lil' Pete", a reference to the fact that Dad had the same first name as Gramp, and that he was six foot six and weighed 240 pounds. The massive physique was matched with a massive calm that had similar effects on brawling miners at the Fraser House or the Miners' Home, and on pre-teens caught out after the 9 PM curfew siren. No one tangled with Dad because the entanglement never seemed worth it. Now, as he thought of Dad, Jimmy's high purpose at the Sinkhole seemed to fade away. He grabbed his clothes, but didn't put them on. Harry lived on Cross Lake, and it was only about three hundred yards to the shore.

Once at the lake, he hid his clothes and waded in. Cross Lake was considerably colder than the Sinkhole, and he stood for a time waist deep and shivering before finally ducking under. Then he swam easily across the bay to Harry's dock, about two hundred and fifty yards.

Harry's mother didn't seem surprised to have a dripping boy knock at her kitchen door. She just said, "Hi, Jimmy," and shouted "HARRY!" without a breath in between. It took five minutes and two more yells before Harry appeared in his pajamas.

The two boys fished from the Harry's canoe for two hours, catching a few perch too small to keep, then had wieners and beans on the dock before going out again. Jimmy sensed that it was about three o'clock, and thought it would be fun to be near the high school when the afternoon exam ended. Harry wasn't interested, so Jimmy dove from the canoe and swam to where his clothes were hidden.

The sun had worked its will on his peanut butter and jelly sandwich, and he had to scrape it, mouthful by mouthful, from the waxed paper. Then, putting on his shirt, he realized that he had made an awful mistake. His back and shoulders radiated waves of heat outwards and waves of pain inwards. A day of sitting in a canoe on still water had its price. Now he would go home and his mother would … What would she do? Mom was sort of unpredictable. In lots of ways, she treated him as an adult, expecting him to be as smart out of school as he was in, and that was hard.

Finally he was home. "My God, look at you!" He started to mumble apologies for his stupidity, when he realized she was crying. He was in bed within two minutes, the doctor was called, and his mother began putting oil on his back, touching it so lightly that he tried to compare her touch to his own. The back hurt (later the doctor would call it a "doozy" of a burn), but he felt strangely OK. His Dad was already on shift. With only two policemen in town, one did days one week and nights the next. Dad was on nights this week, and would patrol the town until the beverage rooms closed, then sleep lightly by the phone.

Dad came home for a bite about six, and Jimmy heard Mom telling him about the burn. "Take it easy on him, Pete — he's being pretty brave about it, and I think he knows it wasn't too bright." So when Dad came into the room, he didn't say anything, really. Then he went out to the police car and left to be in evidence downtown between the Miners' Home and the Fraser House. At 6:30 the beverage rooms had to shut down for an hour and a half, and a police presence had a calming effect.

There wasn't much sleep that night, but Jimmy felt a curious sort of contentment, something he tried to explain to himself, but couldn't. Summer had truly begun.

CHAPTER 2

Parksville

I was still staring out over the strait when the clouds cleared dramatically, and the white brightness of the Coast Range flashed its beauty at me. I'd been reaching for a summary memory, if I can put it that way, a sort of précis of that summer of 1949, and instead I'd been presented by my insistent brain with a recreation of one day, and not the crucial day either, just the first day of that summer. I looked at my watch and realized that well over an hour had passed since I came out on the deck. If my memory insisted on going at this thing one day at a time, it would be weeks before I got to the interesting part.

But I guess that summer was about Dad and me, at the core, and maybe that freedom day, the one that ended with excruciating sunburn, explains something. He had just come into the room and smiled at me, no scolding, no reminders of the foolishness I'd shown. Mom too. I was too old for spanking, I figured. I was about to go away to cadet camp. Maybe that sunburn was a little rite of passage, the clearest case I can remember of an action carrying its own consequences. The blisters and the peeling that followed took less than a week, but it was an uncomfortable week, and took away much of the freedom my scholarship had earned. Exams were over before I even got over to the High School to sit on the lawn and gloat.

It's easy to forget how hard my parents worked. Two cops in a town of over two thousand, a town with a rowdy history and rough manners. The man on night shift slept at home, where the telephone operator would route all calls, but he was still on duty for sixteen hours a day for the seven days. That week, Uncle Jim (no real relation but close enough that I thought of him that way) was on days, and he did the office work down in the town hall. Both of them got a week off in the summer, with an OPP officer shipped in from North Bay to cover.

Mom worked just as hard. That was the summer before we got an electric stove. There was no vacuum, no washing machine, no drier, no mixer, no electric kettle . A woodpile was replenished once a year, with two weeks of hard labour for all of us, but splitting and carrying were daily chores. The store was only two blocks away, but we carried all purchases: Dad would never dream of using the police car for personal errands.

And yet she got through an amazing number of books. She and a network of friends traded them, and a good novel would go the rounds in a month or so, read by ten or twelve people. Now that Willy was reading too, sometimes the four of us would quietly munch supper, each absorbed in his or her own book. Looking back, I call it quality time.

There's an old truism that a boy will try to marry someone like his mother. Dee wasn't like Mom, not on the surface. Dee's energy always showed through, with her eagerness for new experience, her readiness to up stakes and away. But she did share that quality of knowing, at least knowing me. It often seems that I have to have my guard up, not let anybody know when I feel empty — and, God knows, all my life, or at least all my life since my teenage years, I've felt, fought off, and mostly succumbed to that feeling. And when it comes, or I should say when it settles in for a long stay, then other people don't count a damn for me, but I still have to have them around to tell me that I'm OK. There was a book titled I'm OK, You're OK. My title would be longer: I'm not OK, but you'd better tell me that I am, and if you do, you'll be OK in my eyes, for a little while, maybe. With Mom when I was a kid, and with Dee for all our life together, I could feel real inside, and not itchy on the surface for reassurance.

But back to Cobalt as it was then. My parents were permissive in the real sense of the word, as most parents were. A kid was allowed to be a kid, and while I might be quizzed on why I hadn't done something, a chore, I was seldom asked where I'd been or what I'd done, or how school was. You went out and played, and no one assumed that because you were out of sight you were in danger. So you wandered at will. Willy got lost once, wandering into the bush towards West Cobalt, and was saved because of the friendly persistence of Shep, a mongrel that had attached himself to our family that year. The incident didn't lead to every kid in Cobalt being forbidden to play in the bush. All of us were warned not to play with those shiny little detonators that seemed so common. The three kids I knew of who lost fingers (in one case an eye) were viewed as a little lacking in mental equipment, but there was no crusade to make the world safe for kids who couldn't follow common sense rules.

That freedom is maybe the main reason for my memory getting stuck in its one-day track. And so much of it had to do with water. Cobalt was, and is, a rocky town, with buildings perched on outcrops, maybe three decent lawns in the whole place. But lakes surrounded it: Sasaguinaga, where I learned to swim in the concrete ruins of the Trethewy Smelter, and learned the other essential skill of ridding myself of bloodsuckers with salt; Cross Lake, site of Harry's home and a few dozen others; West Lake; Bass Lake (five miles away and therefore the site of genuine summer cottages) and many more. Now I look at Georgia Strait and marvel at the lilliputian majesty I (or JimmyThen) invested our little lakes with. But it's like a lot of other things in life — as we see more and more wondrous things, our sense of wonder atrophies. Those Coast Mountains shining at me so brightly seem less mysterious than the far shore of Sasaguinaga, where there was reputed to be a cave with bears and robbers in uneasy cohabitation.

The Toronto paper is still beside me. Ken is probably on the ferry now, just pulling out of Nanaimo. Gloria Peet remains a problem. I wish they'd printed a picture of her, though I doubt if it would help much. Suddenly I decide to change and go out to dinner downtown. Maybe Roger would like some Chinese. I gave him a call.

Jimmy woke to find Willy pulling at his blanket. "Hi, Jimmy?" Of course, Willy had been asleep last night when he got in, and he'd been gone for ... twelve days, altogether, ten days of cadet camp and the travel.

"Yeah, OK, Will, I'm awake."

"How was it?" In Willy's mind, "it" must mean everything, being away from home, living in H-huts with hundreds of other guys, travelling hundreds of miles on trains, seeing the world.

"It was great, Will. I'm going to go next year. and for the long camp. They teach you to drive." It was practically the same words he'd said to his father as they walked up the hill from the station. The train had pulled into Cobalt about an hour before midnight, and he'd been standing beside his kitbag when Dad's huge hand descended on his shoulder.

"Gone for a soldier, Jim?"

"Hi, Dad. It was fun. But good to be home."

"Well, let's get there then. We both need our sleep." dad was on day shift, he guessed, because he was dressed in shirt and civvy pants. They trudged up the hill together, Jimmy spilling over with an endless stream of "and thens". Over by the Fraser House, Uncle Jim was sitting in the town police car.

"Hop in, Jimmy. You can bring your Dad." Dad, who was carrying the kitbag as if it were a purse, made a gesture, his hand cutting across his body and back, meant to convey to his partner his disapproval of using the car to drive off-duty men and their children around. Uncle Jim laughed. "Look, Pete, I've just delivered three drunks up to Hundred and Four, for free. Don't tell me I can't drive a returning soldier up the hill." So we got in, and Uncle Jim asked how the camp was, causing a whole new start to the narrative.

Mom had brewed coffee, and there was a heap of oatmeal cookies on the table, with a big glass of milk. She wanted to settle a few details about how well he had eaten. "Bacon and eggs <u>every</u> morning, Mom." He didn't really like eggs that much, and was secretly looking forward to porridge the next morning — army cooks seemed to make oatmeal with a mixture of glue and tiny pebbles. Midway through his description of Toronto's Union Station, he yawned, and they suggested bed.

Dad had already gone down to the police station when he woke and got down to the breakfast table, but Mom seemed receptive to more of the great adventure. "Mom, is Toronto ever big!"

"I know, dear. I grew up there, remember?"

Of course she had, he knew that. What he'd meant was how big it was to him. Besides, she hadn't seen it lately. "When did you leave, Mom?"

"The first time? That would be the summer of '34, when I met Dad at Green Valley. It was a resort near Gravenhurst, and I was a waitress, he was a busboy. Had to take my orders, can you believe that?" She was smiling. "No wages, just keep and tips, but it was better than nothing. He needed it more than me, anyway ..." She broke off.

"Why?"

She seemed embarrassed, whether at him asking, or Willy watching, Jimmy couldn't tell. But one thing about Mom, she never said something wasn't your business unless it truly wasn't. "Well, Dad had left home then. Things were really hard in those days, thousands of people on the move, mostly single men, but lots of young people too."

"What about the end of the summer? Did he go home then?"

"No, he went up to Kirkland Lake. The gold mines ran all through the depression, cutting wages of course, but always kept working. And he was awfully big for his age." Jimmy was calculating hard. Last month, at Dad's birthday, there'd been thirty-one candles. 49 take away 31 was 18, Dad was born in 1918. So in 1934 he was sixteen, and Jimmy was born in 1936, March, so ... His mother was watching him, and as usual she guessed his train of thought. "We wrote lots of letters. He came down to Toronto the next year to see me, in April, and, well, we decided to get married. We caught the train up to Kirkland Lake, and the next year, along came James Robert Thorpe."

Who was now thirteen and getting very curious about this business of people getting married and having children. He blushed. "Did you get married in Toronto?" He pictured the bride at the doors of Union Station, the groom and the priest waiting by the big clock.

"No, in Kirkland Lake. My father ... well, he didn't like the idea, at my age, and a Roman Catholic..."

The two biggest and most substantial churches in Cobalt, separated only by language, were Catholic, and Jimmy found it hard to believe that members of Protestant churches, those little buildings, could disapprove of his mother moving up in the world. Of course, there had been that church parade at Camp Ipperwash, where over a thousand had lined up on the Protestant side opposite the few hundred Catholics. Now he remembered Mom talking about her father, who had been a Canon in the Anglican Church. Jimmy had always pictured a big artillery piece belching fire, and from her description he wasn't far wrong. His grandfather had visited Cobalt early in the war, when Dad had gone overseas, just before Willy was born, and had made peace with his daughter. He had died in 1945, before VE day, and Mom had gone to the funeral, leaving the two boys at home with Mrs. Keefe coming to stay with them.

"Was Gramp mad at Dad because of you getting married?"

"Oh, no. They fought over something long before. It was after your Aunt Evvy left home, that would be in '33, and your Dad and Gramp just couldn't get along. They still can't, and there's no point in trying to make them. Gramp was always trying to be kind to me, you know, and after the Algonquins mobilized, he gave us that house over on Ruby Street, not much of a house, but we needed something, so you and I came down to Cobalt." She got up abruptly for more coffee, and Jimmy sensed that the information session was closing. Anyway, this was old stuff, and he had fresher news of the world to pass on to friends.

He tried three houses, and the only guy in was Brian. Brian never wanted to talk about anything but his father's new car, year after year. Since this was July, Brian was still in full flush, the new Chevrolet having arrived from North Bay only a month ago. Along about Christmas, Brian would switch over to talking about the new Chevrolet his father was planning on ordering. Jimmy snuck in a few essential facts about Camp Ipperwash, but it wasn't as satisfying as he had hoped.

Roy Laliberte was weeding the garden across the street, and Jimmy helped him for a while. Roy, who was sixteen, said he'd been to Ipperwash the year before, and Jimmy was surprised the two of them had never talked about it, living so close to one another.

At noon, he went back to the house. Mom had a big pot of soup on the stove, tomato with those impossibly fat macaroni in it. She was out in the back, weeding her garden. Jimmy wondered if she'd seen him helping Roy, and he went out to help her. After a while, he asked, "Mom, was Aunt Evvy Dad's little sister?"

"No, she was older, by about a year, I think. I never met her — she just left home like lots of kids did. Gramp got some letters from her for a few years, the last one from out west, Vancouver, I think. We put some ads in the Vancouver papers two years ago, but there were no answers." She straightened up with her hands low on her back. her elbows sticking back. "Let's have some lunch. I think I heard Willy come in the front."

All three of them had two bowls each. Dad usually made it for lunch, but anything could have held him up, so lunch was never delayed for him. Willy couldn't have taken that. Jimmy wondered about Aunt Evvy. This must have been only the fourth or fifth time he'd heard her name, and the picture in the album of Gramp, Nana, Evvy and Dad was one of those ones where the photographer had run around and fussed until everybody was stiff as boards.

Thinking about the picture reminded him of Nana and Gramp. They'd like to hear about camp and the trip and his plans for next year. "Mom, I've still got two dollars left from my travel money. OK if I go up to see Nana and Gramp?"

She shot him a hard glance. "You're not getting on some hobbyhorse about Evvy, are you?"

"Oh, no, nothing about her. Nana wanted me to come see her as soon as I got back." This was true. The money wasn't the point. Gramp always tried to give him some money, once even five dollars, but Jimmy had learned from his father that he shouldn't accept it. Bus fare from Nana was OK. Whenever he came back from Haileybury, where they lived, Dad had this strained look on his face, and it had to be about Gramp. Gramp never visited them, though Nana would drive down once or twice a month, and Dad was always happy to see her. But he never asked about Gramp. Last Christmas, Nana had insisted that they all come up to Haileybury in her car to see her tree, and Dad had gone along. It was the only time in a year that Jimmy could recall the two of them being in the same room.

McIsaac's Bus Lines had the route between Cobalt, Haileybury and New Liskeard, leaving Cobalt on the even hours. Jimmy had no trouble getting downtown for the two o'clock bus, and promised to be back by eight — it was assumed that Nana would feed him. There were about twelve people in the bus, and Jimmy knew half of them by name. None of them were likely to be interested in where he'd been for the past two weeks, so he just looked out the window as the bus lumbered through the windings of Lang Street, then across the bridge over the T.& N.O. tracks. Ahead was the rock face where someone had, at the risk of life and limb, painted six foot high letters saying "JESUS SAVES", and an equally foolhardy jokester had added "BOTTLE CAPS" below it. Jimmy didn't think much of either painter. The first was probably a show-off with what Father Delaney called spiritual pride, and the other was making fun of religion.

The bus chugged and shook over the hill by the O'Brien Property, and accelerated downhill to Hundred and Four, stopping opposite the casket works. North Cobalt was next, the bus running beside the abandoned tram line it had replaced. Then came the first glimpse of Lake Temiskaming glinting in the afternoon sun. Jimmy, fresh from the wonders of Lake Huron, which you couldn't even see across, was not impressed.

Gramp and Nana's house was on the lakeshore, about three blocks from downtown Haileybury. Gramp was proud of the house. He'd bought the lot right after the big fire that had levelled Haileybury in the early twenties, and he had built a house that rivalled any in the "Millionaires' Row" that had gone up in smoke. Everyone in the two towns agreed that Gramp was a smart man with a dollar, and there was a lot of guessing about how many of those dollars he had. He had come into the Cobalt camp with the first rush in 1903 as a young man, and by the First War, he had made himself important, working as manager of several mines, including the Coniagas, and the Nipissing. He knew everything going on in the camp, and he bought shares in the mines that were going somewhere. Then, in the mid twenties, he got right out of Cobalt mining shares, just before the world price of silver nosedived, and half the mines closed down. He kept his gold shares, premium mines in Kirkland Lake, V-Town, and Timmins, saying that gold would be solid, and it was.

Jimmy walked to their house, rehearsing in his mind their pleasure and astonishment in seeing him. Gramp was on the porch in a rocker, and Jimmy crept up the lawn, the steep terraces hiding him from view of the porch until he was able to scramble up the stairs shouting "Hi, Gramp!"

"Jimbo! Good to see you, boy. Catherine! Guess who's here?" and Nana came bustling out to grab him and hug him. About five years ago, by silent agreement, they had settled on a dignified hand-shake as the best way of showing respect in both directions. Jimmy went over and offered his hand which the old man shook. Soon there was a big jug of Freshie with ice cubes, there were cookies, and the three of them were sitting around the big cast iron porch table. It was Jimmy's most satisfying audi-ence of the day, barring Willy, who could be held spellbound by anything.

When the phone rang, Nana started to get up, but Gramp stopped her. "It'll be that fool Ferguson. I told him to call about now." and he got up to go and berate his long-suffering broker for doing some-thing or for neglecting to do something. Jimmy looked at Nana, and had an impulse to ask her about Evvy. He smothered the impulse, partly because he had as much as promised his mother not to raise the subject, but also because of a memory of last Christmas, when Dad had said something about Evvy. Nana's face had just crumpled up. Grams had gotten red in the face and had rumbled something at Dad, who was already holding Nana and patting her back.

Nana, unaware of how he was picturing her face that time, asked, "How's your Dad? That town works him too hard, you know. Haileybury is the same size, and a whole lot quieter, and we've got three police officers." Jimmy already knew this. Everyone in the two towns was kept aware of deficiencies and differences. The only thing they could agree on was a mutual hatred of New Liskeard, double the size of either of them.

"Fine, I guess. He picked me up at the station last night, and Uncle Jim drove us home in the police car. Dad went to work early this morning and I missed him." Jimmy leaned back and looked out over Lake Temiskaming. Gramp and Nana's house was huge compared to his house, and it looked rich. He remembered Mom saying how Gramp had given them the house on Ruby Street, and he also remembered how that house had split in two one winter, the winter after Willy was born. The roof had stayed intact, but the side had cracks that widened to a good foot and a half at the top. They stuffed the cracks with everything they could find to get through the winter, though Jimmy wondered now if blocking the air made much difference, The only heat in the house was the kitchen stove, and the kitchen was sort of an add-on to the main house. Here in this house was solidity, a porch that didn't creak under your weight, huge pillars, five bedrooms upstairs, a formal dining room big enough for twelve, but never holding more than two or three, and a basement with one of the wonders of the world, an automatic oil furnace.

Suddenly he felt anger at Dad. Running away from all this at fifteen was one thing. Every teenager had fights with his family. But Dad was stubborn, too stubborn. And unfair. Whatever Gramp had said to him back then, he'd never hurt him since Jimmy knew anything about it. Mom's father had come up to Cobalt to make up with her, and she'd accepted it. He looked at Nana again. She must long for her son to come home again, as she did for her daughter, the lost Evvy. But Dad was stubborn.

CHAPTER 3

I don't know how much of that was dream and how much thought, or where there is a dividing line. It's all true, I know that — there was none of the exaggeration of dream, it happened just like that, my day, or rather Jimmy's day back in July of 1949. After I got up, I checked my perpetual calendar. 1949 has the same setup as 1994, so my wall calendar for this year is just as good a reference. Jimmy got home on a Friday night, almost certainly the fifteenth of July, so what I have just relived through his eyes was a Saturday.

What is both annoying and frustrating is that I don't seem to have any control over this memory. When it starts up, that is, when Jimmy wakes up, I run through his day with him, without any opportunity to edit, to cut to a later time, to fast-forward. What's the use of hindsight if I can't use it to leap ahead? But no, I'm stuck watching this film-like progression. And the detail! If someone had asked me yesterday where the bus stopped in Hundred and Four, I would have been stumped.

I'd put it down to something I ate, but Roger and I were quite conservative, ordering the dinner for two. Nor did I get overtired, climbing into bed at a quarter to ten. In fact, I'm sure that I woke fully before the memory really took over. Gloria Peet. I'm pretty sure I owe her no responsibility, for she had her fun in Toronto and other cities, totally unaware that she should be mouldering (at last) in a grave in the Catholic cemetery, just off Highway 11 between Hundred and Four and North Cobalt. That she wasn't there seems vaguely (to me) her fault, since I (or Jimmy, I should say) and so may others were convinced that she was laid to rest, at last, that summer of '49. To last till the summer of '94 seems perverse.

There is one bright spot in this situation. My memory is not determined to drag me through the summer day by full-blown day. It seems to be selecting some high points to play back to me in detail. There's not much mystery to me why this Saturday came back. Mom, of course, is one reason. Do other people feel the same way about their mothers, that they know their children so thoroughly that the child barely needs to speak? I know that's a common feeling in childhood, but I still feel it about her. Some of my friends are lovingly, indulgently, sure that their mothers don't know very much. Perhaps it's because Mom died in 1956, when I was twenty (and she was less than forty!). But I don't think I have magnified her in my mind. I still feel, and I'm well past forty, that she had a particular wisdom. Part of that wisdom might have been an incuriosity about Dad's family — I don't recall her ever asking him anything directly about Evvy, and, while she seemed to like Gramp on the limited occasions when they saw each other, I never heard her referring to him while talking with Dad. Nana yes, Gramp no.

Her own mother died in a tragic accident when she was in her early teens, and she was left in constant touch with her autocrat of a father, a touch which rubbed both of them raw. Her assertions of independence, I learned later from her sisters, had an epic quality to them, and they were crowned by elopement with a Catholic. This sounds like a recipe for disaster, and I don't doubt that hundreds of similar cases have hit the rocks of reality, but in her case it was fulfilment: she was fully and completely in love with Dad, and he with her, until the day she died.

Funny, when I found out about Mom's home life with her father, I was already married. Dee asked me once about Dad and me. I don't even remember what I said, but my hostility must have shown enough that Dee backed away immediately and forever. I wonder if the power to heal, so strong in both Mom and Dee, comes partly from a recognition of limits. Mom knew, basically, what separated Dad and me, and if she hadn't died when she did, could probably have cured both of us. Dee never knew the story, and my not telling her just shows that I didn't trust her enough. I should have.

I put some coffee on and began to think about breakfast. It would never get as hot on this island as it was in Cobalt and surroundings that year. Today, however, promised sun. Already, there were white sails dancing out in the Strait in light winds and low waves. That tabloid paper which started the whole thing was on my deck chair. I picked it up and gave it a savage twist. I went down the steps and along to the big green garbage can I keep there, mounted on big wheels like a golf cart. The paper thunked into the empty garbage can.

Jimmy stretched in his bed and winced. His muscles were sore, all right, and he wished it were Monday again, the Civic Holiday, but no, it was Wednesday, the fifth of August, another workday. He and the guys had taken Monday off, and gone down to Bass Lake for the Kiwanis picnic and fair, because customers wouldn't be home anyway. But yesterday, they'd had to work hard to catch up.

He wondered if Charlie was sick of the Nugget route yet. He'd passed the route on to him for the summer, to get free for cadet camp, but, knowing Charlie, he'd expected to get it back when he returned, because Charlie never stuck at <u>anything</u>. He'd waited, and then finally asked outright, but Charlie just hemmed and hawed, saying maybe he'd take the last two weeks of August off, see him than. No paper route, no money.

It was almost three weeks ago that Roy Laliberte came up with the idea of selling ice. Roy had two passports to the adult world, a driver's licence and the use of his uncle's half-ton, the uncle being out in the bush somewhere on a diamond drill rig. That day, Roy had called to Harry and Jimmy as they sat on the porch steps of Jimmy's house. "Hey, you guys wanna make some cash?"

"Do fish wanna swim?" Harry answered, and Jimmy thought about that for a second — do fish really <u>want</u> anything? But they were both off the porch steps and across the road pretty quickly. Roy leaned against the side of the half-ton. Jimmy kicked the rear tire, but lightly. Harry ran his fingers through the dust on the fender. The old Ford had those flaring fenders from before the war. Harry's fingers uncovered no gleam, just a dull brownish red.

"Y'know the Gibson Property, that open cut?" This was like asking them if they knew where Galena Street was; the Gibson Property was only about 400 yards from where they were standing, and the big open cut on it had been adventure country for years. There had been over a hundred mines in Cobalt in the boom years from 1903 to about 1927, many of them completely forgotten except by the mining recorder's office up in Haileybury. About five mines were operating now, 1949. Few mines went deeper than seven or eight hundred feet, because the silver just ran out here, at what they called the Diabase Layer. That meant the whole town was sitting on rock that must have looked like Swiss cheese. That time Jimmy's house out in the Wright Subdivision, the one on Ruby Street, had split apart, it was because of some cave-in far below in an abandoned mine.

The Gibson Property took up much of the hill called the Little Buffalo. You got to it from the northwest, because it was fenced on the town side.There was a softball diamond down on the hard flat cyanide slimes between the Little Buffalo and the Big Buffalo, a taller hill holding Cobalt's cylindrical water tower. Jimmy had been amazed in Camp Ipperwash to see softball played on grass, and even more amazed to hear that this was normal. Anyway, if you stood where first base was normally put and looked well to the left of home plate, you could see a trail going past some poplars towards the Little Buffalo. There were no bleachers to block the view - spectators sat on rocks behind home plate or on some logs down the first base line. At the end of this trail, the Gibson open cut began.

He turned his pillow over and bunched it up. Five more minutes, just five. He remembered the day Gramp had explained to him about open cuts.

Last summer, Mom and Dad had gone away for a few days of Dad's week-long summer vacation, and Nana had asked that the boys stay with them in Haileybury. Mom had agreed readily, and Dad gave in. Jimmy had gotten clear instructions. Willy and he were to sleep in the same room so that Willy wouldn't get scared. He was to keep Willy with him unless Nana wanted to take Willy somewhere. Nana, Dad repeated. As it turned out, Willy had spent most of his time with Nana, the two of them walking uptown, visiting her friends, her showing off her grandson who lived only five miles away, but .... Jimmy was with Gramp every day, and most of their time was spent in and around Cobalt. It was odd. Jimmy was used to seeing Gramp in the house in Haileybury or on the porch. Gramp never came to Cobalt, but now he wanted to be there three days in a row.

The first day, Jimmy recalled them meeting an old guy near the post office, "Well, if it ain't Pete Thorpe. Come down to the old town, eh?" Keep askin' Li'l Pete how come you never visit, and he don't say boo." And Gramp had talked to the old guy for almost twenty minutes.

As Gramp and Jimmy got back into the big black Buick, Gramp said, "Used to be a shift boss in a mine I managed back in '25-26. Good man back then. Says your Dad does a good job down here."

"You know he does, Gramp." Gramp just grunted, and the two drove around Cobalt Lake out to the old Nipissing Property. In a few minutes, they were standing on some piled rocks, looking into a sharp vertical canyon, about ten feet wide, winding back into the hill until it came to a sudden halt at a rock face about thirty feet high.

"Y'see here, well, there was some silver show, probably right on surface, scrape away some moss and there'd be that little gleam. Lots of places didn't even start off with a shaft, just a few guys hand steeling to bench down and follow a vein. So you see some of these open cuts, they got started that way, a little operation, drill down and blast, then use a slasher to pull the muck out. But you can't go far that way. Vein's still looking good, or say you get a drill core hundred feet down or so, in the long run it's best to sink your shaft and drift out to where the vein is, then stope, drill up and blast, let gravity handle your muck. Well, a lot of these little operations stoped up till they just had a little shell of rock for a roof, and eventually, that fell in. Those are the deeper cuts, and most of them hook onto drifts that go to a shaft some where, Nobody knows where all the workings are, cause once you started a mine, you didn't have to tell anyone where you were going underground, long as you were within your surface claims. Don't you go fooling around in any of those old workings. They're mighty tricky, timber's rotten in them, and the ice has been working on the rock, so it's rotten too."

Jimmy winced at the memory and turned over in his bed. He had been warned, sort of officially. Dad had known that he and Harry had gone into open cuts, but not far. There wasn't a kid in Cobalt who didn't explore a bit, and what is more enticing than a cave? Dad had simply said to be careful, the same way he would have warned about danger in making a tree house. But now Roy was proposing something tricky.

"You know how the ice houses are going?" Roy asked, tossing the keys to the half-ton and catching them. Harry and Jimmy nodded. Both of them lived in houses with electric refrigerators, and in fact, refrigerators were becoming the norm in Cobalt, maybe two thirds of the houses having them. It was definitely the first appliance any housewife wanted. But there were still many houses that depended on ice being delivered every second day.

The iceman would come with his horse and wagon, the ice under big sheets of burlap in the back. The horse, just as clever as the milkman's horse, would stop at the next customer. On Nickel Street, there were eight customers, including the Lalibertes. The iceman would haul a big block out from under the burlap, and with four or five swift strokes of his icepick, break off a smaller block that would fit precisely the ice compartment of the customer's icebox, The tongs would be casually flung at the block, some- how catching the exact point of balance, and the iceman would, equally casually, carry the block in, holding one handle of the tongs. The horse, sensing the weight of the block leaving the wagon, would let out his clutch and amble on to the next customer, with little kids chasing to catch the little chips of ice left on the tailgate. Brush off the sawdust, and there was your cold treat for the morning.

But this year, as Roy said, the icehouses were in trouble. They had hired men in January or February, just as in normal years, to go out on the lakes and cut ice with long saws. The ice had been put into the insulated icehouses with their heavy doors, thick roofs and banked walls, the ice covered in saw- dust, a normal year's supply. But this year was abnormal. Summer had begun in May, and demand for ice shot up early, people stopping using the space between windows and storm windows for cooling, and verandas as freezers. At the same time, icehouse owners saw their inventory melting away in heat their insulation hadn't been designed to handle. The result was a definite shortage of ice by mid July. Refrigerator owners tried to help. Right then, one shelf in Mom's fridge was set aside for the Lalibertes, and it was common for Jimmy and Willy, sitting at the breakfast table, to see Mrs. Laliberte come in the door, extract a bottle of milk from the fridge, and hustle back out without a word. Caravello's grocery, the one across from the Fraser House, was in an old head frame, with the shaft accessible from a trap- door in the back, and old Caravello had installed a dumbwaiter system which lowered his butter down about a hundred feet to year-round cool space. Now, many of his customers claimed space in the shaft for their own storage, Mr. Caravello only insisting that the goods be bought from him in the first place. A boy, despatched from the dinner table to get butter, would find himself travelling three or four blocks to the store, nodding at Mrs. Caravello on his way to the back, climbing down the ladder in near darkness, finding his family's box, and climbing back up with the right amount of butter.

But still there was a shortage of ice, a seller's market that an entrepreneur (Jimmy had learned that word in the spring, and used it whenever he could, which wasn't often) like Roy would recognize and exploit. "Y'know, there's ice in that Gibson open cut."

"Not this year, Roy." Jimmy had been into the open cut the week before, and where there was normally a gleam of ice back in the drift, there was only the shine of water.

"Deeper there is."

Yes, probably there was. After about a hundred to a hundred and fifty feet into rock, it doesn't matter how hot he surface is, you are into the climate of eternity. And that climate, until you go deep enough for the rock to heat up, remains forever below freezing unless there is enough human activity, fires, lights, blasting, working bodies, to warm the air there. In a non-working mine without much air circu- lation or too much water seepage from the surface, ice will form at these levels and stay forever. Jimmy had this on Gramp's authority.

"Well, all we gotta do is go down there, chop ice, and haul it up. I'll deliver it in the half-ton. We can charge double the usual price." Roy was right. That had been the beginning of a joint enterprise for the four of them, Jimmy, Harry and Andy, Roy's younger brother, working on extracting the ice, and Roy selling it. Jimmy suspected that Roy was maybe collecting more than he showed them at the end of each day, but still, eight hours of fairly hard work would net each of the underground workers almost two dollars. Roy kept four (he said) because of the cost of gas.

Jimmy rolled over in his bed again, and his back muscles screamed at him. He didn't want to go down in that cut again. The first time had been an adventure. Back in the drift, before they lost the light of day, they had lit their little lanterns. Harry, whose father worked at the Silver Miller, had brought an old hard hat and a carbide lamp, but Jimmy and Andy just had candles in tin cans, with flashlights for emergency use. Later, Jimmy had "liberated" an old coal-oil lamp from the back shed, a vast improvement over the candle. Now, the first day, Harry started the water drip in his carbide lamp, and lit the acetylene flow with a whoosh.

They found a raise going down about thirty feet back of the farthest point Jimmy had been before, with an iron ladder. Roy went first, then Harry for illumination. Fifty feet down the raise, maybe two hundred feet from the top of the Little Buffalo above them, they saw their first ice, and then emerged into a stope with lots of ice. They had all brought hatchets, and they hacked off a few chunks, put them in their bags (Jimmy's army kitbag was ideal as long as you remembered not to fill it too full), and climbed back up. Then back for more.

The next day, they got more efficient. Roy found an old pulley and rigged a little tripod at the top of the raise, A person below could haul up a bigger chunk of ice than he could carry on his back, and bigness was desirable. Roy said the little chunks they got the first day had just about melted by the time he got them to customers. A division of labour began: Jimmy, who had brought a full sized axe from the back shed, plus the lantern, hacked away at the ice. Harry hauled it to the raise in an old wagon, and worked the pulley. Andy grabbed it at the top, and piled it under burlap until Roy came back from a trip. Then he and Roy would load it in the truck while Jimmy and Harry rested a bit. Then start cutting the next load.

Still lying in bed, Jimmy thought of how tiring it was, how tiring it was going to be. And he worried about how honest he was being with his parents. Dad knew about the ice enterprise, of course. He knew everything that went on in Cobalt. But Jimmy knew he assumed they were cutting up where the ice had always been in previous years, up in the drift going straight into the hill. He could picture Dad in the police car, seeing Roy go by in the old red half-ton, and thinking he might just go over to the Gibson Property and have a look at things. The whole enterprise would come crashing down then. Jimmy almost wished it would happen, but he wasn't quite sure about the personal consequences. He could handle the loss of income, but there was a definite possibility of loss of freedom as well.

Well, if he had to go, he had to go. He got heavily out of bed and dressed. He had a work sweater and some wool pants over in the drift. It was cold down there.

CHAPTER 4

The little sneak! He started off with the morning of August fifth, and I know what's going to happen that day, but of course I'm not allowed to jump ahead, I'm not in charge of my own memory, and what happens? Zilch, nada, nothing at all. The whole thing is him lying there in bed thinking of not going to work, and remembering a bunch of things. I hope we don't get into one of those hall of mirrors things where I'm remembering him remembering an earlier him who's remembering … I don't think I could take that.

My first reaction when I snapped back to the present was that Jimmy was trying to avoid the issue, maybe feeling some premonition, some foreknowledge of what's going to happen in that old mine that day. But if there's any mind trying to slow it down because it knows what's coming, it must be my own mind — he just doesn't know.. But I've remembered this a thousand times, told many people about the time I discovered Gloria Peet, or the thing that used to be Gloria Peet, the thing I thought was Gloria Peet for forty-five years. So why the reluctance, what is Me-Then-Jimmy trying to tell me? Maybe it's that reality has a richness of circumstance, that important things cannot be compressed into three minute anecdotes to make friends shudder. His thoughts that morning tell some things about Cobalt that are important to the rest of the story, and maybe a few things about Jimmy.

The ice shortage was real, and the reaction of people in Cobalt is interesting. I mean the sharing. Mining towns are like that. For instance, we — our family — had a position in town, Dad being one-half of law enforcement, Mom popular, well read etc. But we didn't occupy a niche in any particular social stratum because the town simply wasn't stratified. People were looked up to in particular contexts, but that didn't confer social superiority on the family. Haileybury was different. The south end of Haileybury was generally French, and they might have had social distinctions, but the north end would not have been aware of them. Within the north, or English, end, there were definite layers of society. Gramp and Nana stood high because of his money and his house on the lakeshore. They didn't golf, but were automatically invited to parties at the golf club, whether they came or not. There were people in Haileybury who kept pieds a terre in Toronto, something that would have you laughed out of Cobalt. To have a neighbour use a shelf in your refrigerator would have been unusual in Haileybury and almost unheard-of in North Bay.

Roy Laliberte. Jimmy called him an entrepreneur, and I can't think of a truer description. He saw a market niche, organized the elements of land (ice in the mine), labour (three younger kids) and capital (his uncle's truck), and in true capitalist fashion skimmed a little and fudged the books. I wonder where he is today? I'll have to look more carefully at the Globe Report on Business.: he may be running some large scale enterprise now. Or scams on the Vancouver Stock Exchange.

It's interesting that Jimmy feels that guilt about deceiving his parents, even implicitly. Kids were remarkably free in Cobalt, maybe everywhere, in 1949. You had to draw your own line between adventure and foolhardiness. Now, there's the sense that if you get by the pedophile on the corner, it's only to be gunned down by a drive-by shooter down the block. In Cobalt, forty-five years ago, there was one poor creature who was widely assumed to be homosexual, and was therefore widely shunned; but now I see that he was harmless, just poor at camouflage. Certainly our parents would not say to be afraid of him, to cross the street if you saw him coming. They just never mentioned him. We kids were free to dream up our own cruelties. What I mean is that kids were able to discover their world without all the cautionary maps that parents today feel they must instil in their children's minds..

That is not to say that abuse, including sexual abuse, did not exist. Some physical abuse of children was simply what some tired miner considered normal discipline, a repeat of what his father had done to him. Sexual abuse, like most things sexual, was undercover. It may have been a hypocritical society, but it did allow those children who were not victims — and victims were, I'm convinced, a small minority — to grow up in a healthy innocence. I know that Jimmy's sexual fantasies at the time consisted of imagining a particularly glamorous girl in Grade Ten consenting to kiss him. Further than that he couldn't really imagine.

His relationship with Gramp? Well, Dad certainly didn't want Willy or Jimmy in close proximity, but he would never articulate reasons. Gramp was in his late sixties then, and whatever had caused the rupture with Dad was well in the past. Notice how Jimmy liked riding in that big black Buick, in spite of his scorn of Brian's boasting about his father's cars. There was a reflected glory from Gramp, and Jimmy liked it. I've become a reverse snob about cars, and perhaps it's because I could never afford a car that would set me as far above the common herd as much as that Buick could in Cobalt.

Well, the next surge of memory will come, I'm sure of it, in living colour and stereophonic sound, and I'm bracing myself. After years of stylizing the story, reducing it to off-beat anecdote, reality will be strong stuff.

Roy liked to drive the half-ton with a panache that his uncle might not appreciate, but his partners/employees loved. Standing in the back, clutching the top of th cab, Harry and Jimmy swayed, laughing as Roy swerved back and forth on the flat slimes, raising a plume of grey dust in the still summer air. Then he braked hard, knocking the wind out of them. Andy was braced against the tailgate. Then Roy took the truck up the trail until the poplars narrowing stopped progress.

Jimmy left the lantern and work clothes in the drift every afternoon, but he had to take the axe home. He also had to keep the supply of firewood up at home so his mother would not notice that the axe was being pressed into other service. He trudged into the drift, pulled on the work pants and sweater, and followed Harry to the raise. Andy got the rope into the pulley while they lit their lamps. Jimmy went down the ladder first, axe and lantern in one hand, his left hand sliding down the rusty iron rail of the ladder, his feet feeling for that missing rung that had almost caused him to fall last week. Harry's carbide lamp hissed above him, and, looking up, he could see how much brighter its circle of light was. Gramp had a lot of old mining gear in the basement. Maybe there was a carbide lamp he could use.

They had made serious inroads into the ice in the past week, and it was dripping now as it hadn't when they first found it. Their lamps, their working bodies, were making the temperature in the stope go up. It was strange to think that, even if it were January or February outside, that drip would continue.

Jimmy had to clamber over some rocks to get to the ice face, rock that had probably fallen as loose from the ceiling of the stope some time in the twenty odd years the mine had been closed. Some more rocks might be up there right now, made unstable by moisture seeping into crevices, freezing and prying the rock out, making it ready to respond to vibration, even noise. Twenty, thirty, even a hundred tons of rock might fall any day of any year. Not August fifth, 1949, thought Jimmy. Prayed Jimmy.

The ice buildup was five to seven feet high, and pretty well extended to the walls of the old stope. He worked on top first, cutting a trench about six inches deep across the stope. Then he cut in from the face, and used an old scaling bar which Roy had supplied to crack a large chunk free. Sometimes Harry had to help him pry with the seven foot bar. Then they would chop the block to pieces about sixteen inches to a side, about Harry's weight limit on the pulley. Then Jimmy would get up on the ice to trench again, while Harry used the kitbag to get the blocks over to the pulley at the raise.

I happened about eleven o'clock. It was the third large chunk in from the face, and it had cracked quite satisfactorily down as far as Jimmy wanted. The pry bar went down almost two feet, and he thought the chunk would come free pretty easily. No movement. So Harry clambered up to lend his weight and his light. Together, they hauled on the bar, and the crack widened a few inches, then stopped. "Hold it there, Harry." Jimmy reached for his axe. Once before, a piece of wood frozen into the ice had caused something like this. He fished downward with the axe, moving it along the crack. There! He had the obstruction. "Harry, move back a bit, shift the bar about a foot that way, so I can get a swing at this."

The first swing was off, and the axe head went below the obstruction. the axe handle jarring Jimmy and making his hands tingle. He stepped back a few inches and swung again. This time he felt the axe bite in. It came out readily, no wiggling needed to free it from the wood down there. The next swing cut right through, and the ice chunk broke free suddenly, the scaling bar coming loose and Harry dumped on his rear end. Jimmy grabbed the bar and moved around to lever the big chunk off the ice shelf. Sometimes they broke into convenient pieces on hitting the rocks. This one didn't.

The two boys climbed down from the ice shelf and prepared to break it up. The bright circle of light from Harry's lamp moved along the chunk and they both gasped at the same time. An arm, two thin bones surrounded by dark brown skin, protruded about an inch from the ice.

It wasn't a dog or a deer, certainly not a bear. The arm was about the same thickness as Jimmy's, and there was no hair. They looked at in in silence for perhaps thirty seconds. "It's an arm," said Harry, hushed.

"See if you can see the other end." Harry moved back and shone his light along the newly exposed ice face. There was the end, not protruding as much, but definitely there, three feet in from the edge of the ice ledge.

"Let's go." The two boys picked their way over to the ladder and began to climb. Jimmy realized that his lantern was still burning on top of the ice ledge, but decided against going back. At the top, Andy greeted them.

"Hey, we should get five or six blocks up here before Roy gets back, and I've only got two."

"Andy, there's a body down there."

"A human body." Harry amplified.

"Holy shit!" The Lalibertes were a little less inhibited in their language than Harry's family or Jimmy's. Andy switched on his flashlight and shone it down the raise.

"It's over in the ice. Frozen in. I chopped off the arm before I knew what it was. let's get out in the air." The three boys moved down the drift to the sunlight, then right out of the cut to where they could sit on the grass. Jimmy breathed deeply, and, for the first time that summer, really appreciated the heat. The mine was colder with the added horror.

"Who do you think it is, eh?" Andy's curiosity was really up.

Harry was annoyed. "Shut up, OK, Andy? We don't know and don't want to find out." That led to a long silence. Andy went over to a small poplar shoot and began to strip it of its leaves. Jimmy thought suddenly, irrationally, of their lunch back at the top of the raise, and decided not to mention it. Harry got up with a quick, jerky motion and walked down the path to where it widened near the slimes. "Where's Roy?"

"Dunno. He was going to a couple of places on Lang Street just before the bridge, but I know he was going to make another pickup before … lunch." Andy got up too. "He should be here any minute." In a few minutes, they did hear the half-ton roaring across the slimes, then slowing to enter the track. Then Roy appeared on the path.

"You guys quitting early?" Roy was developing his foreman skills.

Jimmy let Harry tell him. Andy's face was shining with anticipation. Roy said, "Gimme your flashlight." to Andy, and walked into the cut. Jimmy followed him down the ladder and waited at the bottom while Roy picked his way over to the chunk of ice. The axe was still there, and after Roy had inspected the bit of arm jutting from the block of ice, he took the axe and swiftly split the ice about six inches away from the arm on both sides.

"Bring that kitbag over here," he said, and Jimmy obeyed. He held the bag open while Roy put the small block in it. Jimmy stared at his kerosene lantern, glowing on the ice ledge like a votive candle. Roy let him carry the kitbag to the rope and clip it on to the loop, but helped him haul it up.

"Who'll we take it to?" Jimmy realized that the question was addressed to him, naturally skilled in legal matters as the son of a policeman.

"My place, I guess. Go down the back alley, and I'll put it in our shed. Dad might be home, he's on nights now."

Once the kitbag was deposited in the shed, Jimmy went in to tell his mother. Her only question was "It's still in your kitbag?", and when he nodded, she continued., "Dad's downtown somewhere. I'll call Jim Gardner." She gave the operator the police number, and when Uncle Jim came on, she said, "Jim, the boys have found something. A human arm, they think. No, I haven't seen it yet, it's in a block of ice." A pause. "No, it's in Jimmy's kitbag out in the shed. Roy Laliberte, his little brother, and Harry Bronson were with Jimmy. They're waiting out there." Another pause. "They were cutting ice in that open cut on the Gibson Property." She looked at the ceiling while she listened. "Thanks, Jim. Come along the back alley. The boys will show you." Now she looked sharply at Jimmy. "That wasn't right out in the open cut, was it?"

"No, it was lower down. Down a raise." That part was out now.

She looked at the ceiling again. "Oh, well, it's done now. You know this is the end of your ice business?" Jimmy was wishing his ice business had come to an end yesterday. He nodded miserably. "Well, you go out to meet Uncle Jim at the shed. He'll be there in a minute. I don't particularly want to look at the thing."

The police car came along the alley about three minutes later. Constable Jim Gardner wasn't quite as big as Dad, but had considerable bulk. He looked at the four boys and addressed Jimmy. "Where is it?" Jimmy pointed at the shed, and the policeman moved his arm to usher him ahead. Roy followed them in, and Harry and Andy stayed outside, peering through the door. Jimmy opened the kitbag, rolling it down so that Uncle Jim could see the stump of the arm.

"Hmmm. Looks like you're right. Where did you find it?" Jimmy explained. Now there were two ways Dad could get the news of exactly where the ice was coming from. Well, with a dead body down there, everyone in town was going to know. Uncle Jim was still looking at the stump in the dripping ice block. "With an axe, eh?" Could you see what it was before you cut it?"

"No, i ... we thought it was a chunk of wood holding the ice there."

"Yeah. So the rest of the body is probably down there in the ice, right?" Jimmy nodded. "Well, I think before we go any farther, we'd better make sure this is human." Uncle Jim looked around the shed and picked up the old sledgehammer. "Move your kitbag out of the way."

The block of ice was now fully exposed on the shed floor, and the policeman gave it two tentative taps, then raised the sledge and gave it a definite, but controlled, blow. The ice split, and the arm was exposed. It was a left arm, they could see from the part of the thumb which showed. Most of the hand was still in opaque ice.

"Look at that," breathed Roy.

Jimmy asked, "The skin … could it be a … Negro?"

"I don't think so." Uncle Jim was on one knee, examining the arm, even sniffing. He touched it with his finger. "It's freeze-burn, I think. This is pretty old." Jimmy knew what he meant. When you froze meat, like out on the verandah in the winter, if it wasn't wrapped really well, it got this reddish dry look on the surface. Finally, Uncle Jim stood up and stretched his shoulders. "Roy, you're the oldest. I think you'd better show me where this body is. First, we'll go downtown and pick up Mr. Thorpe. Both of us should be there. The rest of you, go home. Don't talk to anyone about this for today — we don't want a bunch of people gawking at us down there. OK?" They all nodded.

As the police car drove out the alley, Jimmy said, "You OK to go home, Andy?" Andy shrugged his shoulders and started down the side yard of Jimmy's house to the street and home. "Come on in, Harry. We can phone your Mom from here."

They were met at the kitchen door by Jimmy's mother. "You boys wash your hands and faces really well. Take off those work clothes." Jimmy realized he still had the sweater and wool pants on. "I've got some sandwiches ready. I've talked to your mother, Harry, and told her that you boys will be here for a while, that you found something the police are investigating. Now, scoot!"

CHAPTER 5

There were details there I could never have remembered through conscious effort. The exact look of that arm, the nimbus of light from the lantern, the shadows on the walls of the stope as Roy went over to the block of ice. It was like a scene from Tom Sawyer, boys in the cave, Injun Joe. But this was real — I remember the feel of that ladder, my foot waving over the missing rung, the feel of the rusted iron under my hand.

At this point, Jimmy had never heard of Gloria Peet, of course. The arm, the thought of the rest of the body there, was oddly thrilling, so that the boys wavered between horror and excitement. That feeling I remember well. For all the freedom I've been talking about that kids had in 1949 Cobalt, we had definitely gone beyond the limits in going down that mine and chopping ice. — later, I worked underground for a time, and I shuddered at the risks I had taken at thirteen. So, when Dad got around to thinking about me down there, I was going to be in deep trouble. In this, I feel fully at one with young Jimmy. It's funny — no matter what age or wisdom you attain, something you did that was unequivocally wrong will still make you ashamed. When I was twelve, I filched, boosted, lifted — stole a chocolate bar from the Five and Dime, was caught, and reported to my father. At fifty-eight, I still blush slightly at the memory. So I didn't need the cinematic memory to remind me that I was wrong in that ice business, that I didn't have the right to take those risks. Under the excitement, young Jimmy was feeling genuine guilt, and was waiting for the retribution.

Oddly, it never came. Dad did reprimand all of us for the stupidity, but it was a policeman reprimand with none of the special anger that I expected to be reserved for his own son. Mom was quite clear that this was never to happen again, but she was never successful in projecting anger, perhaps because she had, I now see, a finely tuned sense of the ridiculous. But Dad could project anger, and in this case he didn't. Instead, he appeared to young Jimmy to be detached. My hindsight of forty-five years says it was preoccupation.

Jimmy's question about whether the arm was from a Negro was not an example of that late twentieth century sin, prejudice. He had, in his young life known one black person, a boy named Fred at cadet camp. He was aware that many people of that race existed (he was an avid reader of Time and was an indoctrinated Republican for several years, to no purpose), but that was theory. He was no more prejudiced against Negroes, blacks, coloured people, Afro-Americans or Afro-Canadians — than he could be said to be prejudiced against unicorns. His surroundings were multi-cultural in some ways: Cobalt had a Finn Hall, a Ukrainian Hall, a White Eagle (Polish) Hall, a St. Jean de Baptiste Society. There were some DPs, or Displaced Persons, in town, a ripple from the great waves of postwar migrations. Like every northern town, Cobalt had a few Chinese who catered stoically to the tastes of miners, who wanted quantity above everything else. But the multi-cultural Canada of today, with its completely relative view of cultures would have puzzled the most progressive citizen of Cobalt in 1949.

Well, now maybe the re-creations of the past can take a rest. The discovery of the body was, I think, the only significant thing that Jimmy contributed to the drama of Gloria Peet, or whoever she was. True, Jimmy developed some ideas, and came into some conflicts later, but this was the one concrete thing he was really involved in. I'm glad I threw that tabloid away.

The sandwiches were good, and Mom's presence discouraged any conversation about the arm. She asked Harry about his aunt, whom Mom had known years before in Kirkland Lake, asked Jimmy about the Nugget route, when Charlie intended to quit, compared the heat wave to the one ten years before in the summer before the war, asked some questions about Ipperwash which showed she had been listening when Jimmy had been talking everyone's ears off a few weeks before.

It was four when Harry said he'd better be getting home. Jimmy walked with him as far as the top of the hill. They didn't talk about the arm, but did look over at the Little Buffalo, wondering what was happening down below its surface.

Then Harry walked down the hill, and Jimmy turned back towards home. After passing the end of the alley, he stopped and turned, walked into the alley, and stood for a few moments looking at the door of the shed. It couldn't hurt to just look at it again. He glanced toward the house. He would only be in sight of the kitchen window for a second, and he slipped into the shed, pretty sure that Mom hadn't seen him.

The sun was slanting in now through the one window, showing dust in the air, but hitting the arm on the floor directly. The ice was gone, only a puddle seeping into the floorboards. Uncle Jim had touched it, and Jimmy reached out, squatting beside the thing. The skin was papery, like a dry leaf, and there was open space beneath it. He touched it again. The hand was palm up, the brown wrinkled fingers bent slightly. He touched the thumb, then pushed it lightly, and the arm rolled over. There was flash of colour, a bright purple spot on the little finger catching the sun. A ring. Jimmy touched the ring, then held it between his thumb and forefinger.

A dog scratched at the door and whined. Jimmy's hand jerked. To his horror, the ring moved, the whole finger seemed to fall apart, a dry cylinder of papery skin sliding right off the discoloured bone. The ring fell from his fingers. Why couldn't he leave well enough alone?

For a minute, he continued to crouch beside the arm. Dad and Uncle Jim would be coming back sometime, and one thing they would be bound to do was to reunite the arm with the body. He thought about trying to reassemble the finger and the ring, but his hand was shaking. He pressed it to his side to control the trembling, then reached out and picked up the little cylinder of dry skin. There! he had it. Quickly, he slid it onto the bone of the little finger.Only then did he look at the ring and realize that he couldn't get it back on the finger without breaking the skin again.

He thought back to Uncle Jim splitting the ice. The thumb had been exposed, not the whole thing, but the base of it. They had not been able to see any of the fingers. So no one knew there was a ring. All Jimmy had to do was get rid of the thing, turn the hand back to palm up, and no one could tell he'd been in here interfering with the evidence.

By now, the puddle was almost dry, and when he turned the arm back and looked at it, there was no sign that it had been disturbed. The skin was broken on the little finger, but there were cracks in the skin all over the hand, and the little finger didn't look different from the rest. he grabbed the ring and put it in his pocket, then stood up and backed over to the door, half expecting the hand to point at him.

It was Brian's dog, Brownie, outside. he wagged his tail as Jimmy came out, made an attempt to get into the shed, but settled for a few pats from Jimmy. The boy reached down and picked up a stick, and the dog tried to wiggle its hind end off. Jimmy threw the stick, and the dog was off, a brown streak close to the ground. Jimmy walked to the end of the alley. The dog was coming back. If Jimmy threw the ring into the ditch, the dog would be after it, and besides, it seemed … disrespectful. He turned left and walked to the top of the steep steps going down towards the public school. he looked back. Brownie had found something else to do in the alley, or perhaps it was his feeding time.

Under the top of the first flight of the wooden steps, he dug a little hole right beside the first support timber, and shoved the ring down about six inches. Then he patted the earth smooth.

As he passed Bazinets' house on his way home, he realized that his hands and nails were brown with dirt, and they felt unclean even under the dirt. He went to the side of the house and used the outside tap to wash his hands. "What are you doing now?" Mom was leaning over the verandah railing.

"Just getting a drink." Swiftly, he moved his face under the tap,. Now his shirt was sopping wet. "And cooling off." His mother looked at him and sighed audibly. She went inside, and a minute later called his name.

From the kitchen, he saw that the police car was in the alley and the door to the shed was open. "Jimmy, maybe you'd better stick around here in case your Dad has some questions." Her tone was neutral, but he knew his Dad had been down that raise, and that eventually, there was going to be an uncomfortable discussion of risk, responsibility, and common sense. He kept his eyes on the shed door. Then Uncle Jim came out carrying a wrapped bundle. He went to the back of the car. Dad came out of the shed and hurried to open the trunk. He took out a lantern and an axe, and Uncle Jim put the bundle in the run. The two policemen talked for a moment, then Jim got into the car and started it. As it went down the alley, Dad watched it disappear, then stood there staring down the alley. Jimmy started to count. he got to a hundred and fifty-five before Dad turned and started towards the house, leaning the axe against the back of the shed and putting the lantern beside it as he came.

Jimmy waited for Dad to start, but the big man looked at him absently, and turned to Mom. "I've got the night duty tonight and already I'm beat. I'll just wash up, have a bite, and then nap."

Mom threw a glance Jimmy's way, and Dad said, "Oh, yes. Jimmy, go to your room for a minute. Mom and I have to talk." Jimmy thought the jury was going out before he had a chance to plead, but since he had no credible plea, he nodded and walked out of the kitchen.

He could hear Mom as he started up the stairs. "Pete, how dangerous was that place?"

"Pretty bad. Lots of evidence of loose falling over the years, and where some came, more can. We'll have to punish him some way." Jimmy waited for a few seconds, but there was no immediate reply, and if he were caught halfway up the stairs, it would make things worse. In the upstairs hall, below the window at the front of the house, there was a register with a cast iron grate. It wasn't like the registers in Gramp and Nana's house, where hot air rushed up in winter. This one just allowed an air flow between floors, but it had the added advantage for kids of being a listening post. However, they were in the kitchen, and although he could hear Mom's low quiet voice and the deeper rumble of Dad's, he couldn't make out the words. The prisoner continued to his cell.

Dad entered after about five minutes. "Jimmy, do you know how tricky that mine is? You could have been killed anytime in the last two weeks. What were you thinking of?"

"Well, we were after ice, and at first we thought we could get it higher up, but there wasn't any and ..."

"And nobody wanted to chicken out?"

"Yeah, I guess that was it."

"Look, Jim, there's over a hundred old mines in this town. If all the kids dare each other too much, we wouldn't have any kids left. Might make life easier, but for some reason we like having kids around. So mines are *verboten,* got it?"

"Yes, sir."

"And you are not to leave the house or the yard for a week, unless Mom sends you on an errand. Understand?"

"Yes sir."

"And I'm going to have a talk with young Roy Laliberte about child labour laws, safety, and a few other things." The focus was slipping away from Jimmy, and he felt relieved. "Now come down for supper. And don't ever do anything dumb like this again." There went the dream of glory at the Sinkhole, but right now, Jimmy was ready to give up all adventure.

Supper was ham and scalloped potatoes. Jimmy normally felt that he had a right to voice complaints about the way the sauce looked curdled on his potatoes, but this time he decided to imitate Willy, to whom food was fuel, and who never saw a plate he didn't like. After supper, Dad got into his uniform and walked downtown to pick up the police car. At 6:30. the beer parlours closed for an hour and a half, a time the government hoped that beer drinkers would go home to their families. Mainly, the two Chinese restaurants got the benefit along with the risk that words exchanged in the beer parlour would escalate into fistfights and thrown plates of fried rice. A very large policeman in uniform was a deterrent, another word Jimmy had learned from *Time* and was fond of using.

At 8:30, the combination of heat, physical work, and high excitement overwhelmed him, and he went to bed. Willy, whose bedtime was 8, was still partly awake and surprised to see him. Naturally, he wanted to talk, but Jimmy soon convinced him that the both needed sleep.

At ten, or thereabouts, something woke him, a dream, an arm flopping over on a floor. He sat up suddenly. There was a low sound of voices downstairs. Out in the hall, he walked to the front window. The police car was parked outside. It must be Mom and Dad talking downstairs. He knelt by the register.

"Oh, no, no identification yet. Maybe never. It was a girl, maybe in her teens, but hard to say. She must have been down there at least ten years, from before the war. The fire chief and I got most of the ice off her before we got her up to surface. She's over at Belanger's, thawing out. The body's all dried out, sort of mummified. Bet it doesn't weigh more than thirty-five, forty pounds." Mr. Belanger ran the combined ambulance/funeral service in Cobalt with one all-purpose vehicle.

"Oh, Pete, there must be a family that's been wondering about her for all those years!"

"Y'know, Peg, it's amazing. I dropped into the office a couple of hours ago, and pulled the file on missing persons, the ones we originated. If you take the thirties alone, from just Cobalt, there are at least twelve girls reported missing and not cleared later. Then there's all the possibilities from other places."

"What did she look like?"

"Really hard to say. Her face was bashed in, so I think it's foul play — it doesn't look like that happened long after death. Hair was short, original colour not too clear. You know, looking at her after we got her up, I almost thought it could be …" His voice trailed off, and then he cleared his throat. Jimmy heard a chair scrape, and the heavy tread of his father walking to the kitchen, then back. His mother waited. That was her real conversational skill, not saying anything until it meant something and was needed.

"Evvy?" The prompt was quiet, calm.

"Yes."

"Pete, she's not even listed in the missing persons file, is she?"

"No, there were those letters. But there's …something. It's hard to explain, Peg. It's a feeling."

"Sure, Pete, you can't just shut those things down. But be careful. There could be a lot of hurt. Remember your mother last Christmas. I'd keep it very quiet."

"You know, I can't even really remember what she looked like. Isn't that strange? I was almost fifteen when she left, and I guess … well, she was just there, who looks at a sister? I looked at that body today, and tried to think of how big Evvy was. and I couldn't even really guess her height — oh, over five feet, less than five-eight, but that's damn poor estimating."

"It's been what, sixteen years? Don't expect too much of yourself."

"Size is funny, eh? I'm pretty big, been big since I was fourteen. But I have dreams where I'm small, like about nine years old, and I'm there in that house, and I'm scared cause Pa is mad at me … and now I look at him, and he seems sort of shrunk."

"C'mon, there's still some coffee left." Both of them moved to the kitchen where their voices continued. Jimmy lay by the register, thinking, then slipping into sleep.

Willy woke him. He was on his way to the bathroom. "What are you doing here, Jimmy? Walking in your sleep? That's a hard place to lie down." Jimmy shushed him, went back to the top bunk, and slept.

CHAPTER 6

Obviously I was wrong in thinking that these reminiscences, these floods of memory, would end with the discovery of that body. It's not that I had forgotten about the ring. The fact is that I have been ashamed of that impulsive investigation of the arm, and I've never included it in the retellings of finding the body. Also, and I think I'm being honest with myself, I've always been sure that Dad was making too much of the ring after it was eventually found, That he built up a whole structure justifying his own actions on what could have been, probably was, a coincidence.

Right now, I've decided to start keeping a record of this thing. Starting today, I'm going to go back to the beginning, to when I found that newspaper story about Gloria Peet. I've been a reporter all my life, and the reconstruction shouldn't be hard.

This reconstruction doesn't come from some masochistic desire to punish myself. I think it's obvious that Jimmy wasn't into self-flagellation, and that's a constant in my (our?) character. I also have enough journalistic integrity, or hope I have, to keep it from drifting into some apologia pro via sua. In fact, the idea of thinking of Jimmy in third person, the distance I've felt from my younger self, is probably a good thing to continue, not merely as a convention but as a way of keeping some objectivity. Nevertheless, I promise that as soon as I start feeling the sense of identity with my young protagonist, I will signal it in this record by a switch in person. But the little Russian doll, while inside me, is not yet me. There may be other, intervening dolls. Last month, on a walk with Ken, I had to slow down a bit, and I said to him, "I'm not the man I used to be." Well, none of us is. It may be that I could take this narrative right up to a few years ago before I feel that sense of it being myself. I don't know. I do know that within months of that summer of 1949, there were changes in Jimmy which made him a somewhat different person.

As for the ring, it is possible that if it had been left on the finger, some things in the following weeks would have come out differently. Not happily, but differently. Dad might have proceeded more confidently. Maybe it was lack of confidence causing the uncharacteristic bluster and anger which he showed. Or maybe not. If life were a laboratory, we could say, "That didn't work out too well. OK, we'll do it again, changing the independent variable this way. Set it up again." I have read science fiction stories in which the hero is forced to go through the same sequence of events over and over again, until he gets some element of it right and can escape the loop. That's what a lot of fairy tales do — two older brothers have to make mistakes in their quests before the simple youngest brother does it right and wins through.

The simple younger brother to me was, of course, Willy. Willy has, I see, done it right the first time. Not in the material sense, of course. I think he's just getting rid of the mortgage on that little three bedroom rancher, and when he goes to pension, it won't be sending him south every winter. Nor would I say that he is simply happy. He has his frustrations, even tragedies. But Willy is loved. He always has been, by me, by Mom and Dad, by Nan, the quiet woman he married, by his children, his students, everyone who has known him. If Willy had been the one who found that body, who had the ring, somehow he would have done it right, would have handled the ensuing mess with a sure sense of the right thing to do. No one would have questioned his motives, because it is impossible for Willy, even now, to have a bad motive. He just doesn't work that way.

This record is for him in a way, though I'm not sure I'll ever show it to him. If it turns out to be a defence of my younger self or even of the way I am today, so be it. It wouldn't hurt Willy to know (though I'm sure he does) that other people don't have quite the moral compass he has. But it may explain to him, again if he ever sees it, what happened to our family.

Now that my resolve to record them is formed, it may be that the memories will calm down, become more conventional dredging of the past. I'm not sure if I will be disappointed or relieved if that happens.

They went to early mass that Sunday— it would have been August 14 — because it was shorter and before the heat of the day; St. Patrick's was cozy in the winter, with its small windows, not all of which opened. It was just after the elevation of the host that an usher came to whisper in Dad's ear. he shrugged at Mom, and slipped out the side aisle. Jimmy and Willy hardly noticed. It happened often on the weekends Dad was on duty. Mom and the boys would walk down the hill to the church while Dad brought the police car around by road and parked near the church. He would have told Helen Young, the telephone operator on Sunday mornings, that they were off to church and remind her to call Mr. Harrelson. Mr. Harrelson was United Church, but lived right beside St. Patrick's, and would be home during either low or high mass because the United Church service was at 9 AM, right between the two masses. If a call came in for Dad, he would slip into the church and tell an usher. Jimmy sometimes wondered if Mr. Harrelson had to confess to the United Church Minister that he was listening in on a Roman Catholic Mass.

Then he and Willy were at the communion rail. The altar boy, one of the younger ones, held the golden platen under his chin, and Father Delaney murmured "Corpus Christi,"as the wafer was placed on his tongue. On the way back to the pew, he was caught up in the same question as always: if you touched it with your teeth, was that OK? What about if it were stuck to the roof of your mouth. You didn't want to be seen moving your mouth as if you were chewing.

Then mass was over, and he and Willy had to stand around while Mom talked with friends out on the sidewalk. The police car was gone, so Dad had been called to another part of town. Willy was always happy when they went to early mass, having fasted since bedtime the night before. Breakfast delayed was one thing; breakfast omitted entirely was a crisis. Finally, they started the walk home. Breakfast was a treat — cereal out of a box and raspberries.

Nana was there already when they got to the house, putting bowls on the table. They had a seven o'clock mass in Haileybury, where there were three priests, and she had driven down right after mass. Willy ran to her first and hugged her, then Jimmy (who was a little more cautious about this hugging business), then Mom. Nana and Mom turned from the hug to see Willy already seated, spoon in hand. "Not so fast, young fella. Get those hands washed first." In a minute, they were all eating.

"I woke up early," Nana said, "and thought, wouldn't it be nice to have a boat ride on a hot day. Where's Pete?"

"On duty. They called him away from church. That reminds me." Mom went to the phone and cranked it. "Helen? Was it you who called Pete an hour ago?" A long pause, then "Oh, that's all right Helen. Anyone we know?" Finally, "That's a relief, anyway, Bye."

She returned to the table. "A car accident right by the West Cobalt turnoff. Hec Belanger had to take one man to hospital in Haileybury. He just went off the road and into that big rock. Probably from Toronto, Helen thought. It'll likely keep Pete busy much of the day."

Jimmy and Willy watched her. She hadn't reacted to the boat ride invitation. Gramp had a large sailing dinghy, eighteen feet, with a centreboard, and they loved it. When Jimmy was sixteen, he'd been promised, he'd get to sail it himself. Till then, Dad (or Mom, who was the better sailor) had to be in charge. Gramp himself hardly ever went out in it, and Nana, for all her talk about "wouldn't it be nice", meant that for others, not herself. She really didn't like water in large bodies. Mom looked thoughtful for a minute, then said, "I'll leave Pete a note and tell Helen where we've gone. He can't leave town except on a duty call, but he won't mind us going. Maybe he needs some quiet time anyway — the last week has been rough on him."

Nana looked curious, but didn't ask any more. Jimmy knew it must be the body. No final identification had been made, but a consensus was growing in Cobalt that it must be a girl called Gloria Peet, who had gone missing in 1932. her father had died in a mine about five years before, and Gloria was known to be "wild" — though Jimmy suspected that her reputation had probably been exaggerated over the seventeen years. Mrs. Peet, her mother, had indulged thirst after her husband's death until her own death in 1935. She was a regular customer at several blind pigs, there being no legal drinking establishments in mining towns until years later. Picking up his Nuggets the other day, Jimmy had heard old man Orme talking about Gloria Peet: "Pretty as all get out — looked eighteen and acted twenty-one. A real wild one, that Gloria, took up with some traveller, I'll bet. I know I saw her hitch-hiking once, a few weeks before she went missing. We all figured she went a lot farther than the Gibson Mine."

The North Bay Nugget was following the case closely, and they too were betting that it was Gloria Peet. An engineer had inspected the Gibson Property in early 1932, and found very little ice in that stope. Then again in 1935 to find the stope almost full of ice. That narrowed the time frame. The coroner refused to be stampeded; he called her "Jane Doe", the first time Jimmy had heard that term of anonymity. But there were only a few possibilities, and most had been heard from after 1934. As Mom had said, a lot of people were on the move during the Depression, but most either came home or made contact from their new homes before or during the war.

Jimmy had tried to pump his mother on Friday afternoon. "Mom, where did Aunt Evvy go when she left Cobalt in … 1931, wasn't it?

"'33. Toronto, I think was where the first letter came from, two years later. Then somewhere else. The last letter was from Vancouver in 37. Why the curiosity? No, it wasn't Evvy in the mine. I only wish that …"

As usual, when his mother trailed off with an incomplete thought, Jimmy knew the trail could not be followed. Mom never used an incomplete sentence unless she suddenly realized it was going into territory she didn't want to comment on. Any pressing would raise that question again, why the curiosity? And Jimmy didn't want to try any explanation.

Now, on Sunday, they had changed and were in Nana's car quickly. Mom had started to say something about fixing a lunch and Nana had said there was one in her fridge, ready to go into the boat. As they came into Haileybury, Lake Temiskaming glinted in the sun, ninety miles long, the headwater of the mighty Ottawa River, a lake almost nine hundred feet deep in places. Willy was getting excited, bouncing on the front seat beside Nana.

Gramp was on the front porch in his usual spot when they pulled up in front of the house. "Hi there! Where's Pete? Found himself something else to do as usual, eh?" Willy ran up to him and gave him a hug, while Jimmy offered the formal handshake they had agreed on long ago. "Good to see you, Peggy. How's that house in this heat?" They lived in a town-owned house, part of the salary of a police officer. It was reasonable by Cobalt standards, but not much compared with the resurrected Millionaires' Row in Haileybury. Mom just smiled and said that it was warm all right, and we'd try to remember come December.

Then they were in the dinghy. There was an onshore breeze, and Jimmy and Willy took oars while Mom handled the tiller. Soon she had the sail filled, and the boat slanted southward past the town with increasing leeway. There were a few other sails out and a couple of motorboats whining northwards. It was beautiful. Jimmy looked forward and left (port? he wondered) at Burnt Island, the long island in the centre of the lake, part of Quebec. Back and to the left was Dawson's Point a long arm of land reaching miles into the lake. He trailed a hand in the water. It was still cold, even in August of the hottest summer he could remember. Swimming was good in Temiskaming, but the first plunge took courage.

After about an hour, Mom turned the boat into the breeze and spilled the sail They let it flap idly above them and attacked Nana's picnic lunch: egg salad and beef sandwiches, cherries, bottles of Pepsi for the boys, twelve full ounces, that's a lot, cookies, a thermos of coffee for Mom. After they finished, Mom said, "Now the work starts. The wind's come round a bit to the north, and we're pretty far south. We'll have a few tacks before we're home." Her family had had a dinghy on some lake down south, and she had practically grown up on it. Every so often, she would say "Coming around!" and Jimmy and Willy would duck as the boom swung over their heads. The breeze was still light, so the boat didn't heel over too much, but it was fun to see the world twirl before them, the whole horizon sliding around in almost a semi-circle until Mom settled on her new tack,

Jimmy's internal clock told him it was about four o'clock when they neared Gramp's dock. Something else internal was telling him things as well. Willy had tinkled over the side, but Jimmy's problem was more serious, and he told his mother so. "Just jump on the dock and get up to the house," she said. "Willy and I will tie up."

He ran across the highway from the lake side, and up the short street beside Gramp's house. The Cobalt Town Police car was parked there, and he thought Dad had found Mom's note and had come to join them. But right now, his thinking was concentrated on one thing. The side door opened to a hall which had the kitchen on one side and a small washroom on the other, the left side. He got into the washroom. "Just in time!" he thought.

In a moment, he was aware of voices. He couldn't make out the words at first, but he recognized Gramp's rasp and his father's rumble. He looked over at the door to the washroom, and saw that he hadn't fitted the hook into the eye to lock it. He leaned over as far as he could and swung the dangling hook around to fall into the eye. As it clicked down, he realized that the voices were coming from the window of the washroom, a high square one facing northeast, one that was cranked open.

Gramp's voice was angry. "Do you mean to say your first visit to this house in what — eight months? — and you want to look for a letter? From Evvy?" His voice faded and Jimmy couldn't catch the words in the next sentence. The two of them were in Gramp's study, right next to the washroom, and the window there was open too. Then Gramp must have turned around, because his voice got clearer. "You know damned well what's in it, Pete. I showed it to you before you went overseas."

Dad's voice sounded tired, tight, as if he were counting his words out slowly. "Pa, it's just that I've got to be sure … in my own mind, where Evvy was then, in 1937, I mean. She would have been twenty when she wrote it, four years after she … left here." By "here" he meant this house. Jimmy tried hard to imagine a sixteen year old Evvy Thorpe and a fifteen year old Pete Thorpe, Dad, living here. Which bedrooms? What had she looked like? Why did she run away? Mom had hinted that a lot of young people left home trying to find work somewhere else, but this house didn't shout poverty. Jimmy knew that a lot of boys left home at sixteen like his Dad had, and he could somehow understand a boy's decision more.

His Dad was talking again. Now his voice was a little louder and deeper. "Pa, I have to see that letter."

"As a son, or as a policeman?"

"You can take it any way you want. There is an investigation going on…"

Gramp broke in. "You mean that body, that kid — that's Gloria Peet. The paper says so, everybody says so. You think Evvy had some kind of accident and it's her? You're as stubborn as you always were, you and her both. If I were younger, I'd …"

"Hit me, Pa? That ended years ago. OK, if you want it this way, as a policeman, I want to see that letter." There must have been movement in the study because Gramp's reply was muffled. Dad said, "No, I won't be putting it in any file, I don't want it official, can't you see that?"

Something was opened in the study, maybe a drawer in the old wooden desk, a squeak of wood on wood. Then Willy's voice as he ran in the front door. "Jimmy? Where are you?" The squeak of the drawer came again. Jimmy flushed the toilet and began to wash his hands. Willy again:"Nana, why are you crying?"

As he came out of the washroom, he heard Nana and Willy coming from the living room into the kitchen. He crossed the hall and got into the kitchen just in time to meet them there. Mom was only a few steps behind them. She looked at Jimmy "Is your Dad here? I see the car outside."

Nana turned to her. "Why can't he ever come here without a fight starting? What's wrong with them?" Her sobs started again, and Mom moved to take her in her arms.

"I wish I knew, I wish I knew." Jimmy heard feet going down the porch steps, and Gramp shouting something. " ..and sure I tried to knock some sense into you. Never worked."

The police car's engine started, and Mom broke away from Nana, went quickly into the hall, and opened the side door. "Pete! Don't you dare run off now! Stop that car!" The engine died and she let the door close behind her. Jimmy and Willy were staring at Nana, and she suddenly realized it and grabbed a tissue to blow her nose. The two boys moved closer and hugged her at the same time. She almost cried again, but seemed to shake it off with a violent shudder and smiled at them.

Mom found them like that. "It's useless, he won't come in. He's as mad at himself as at his father. Boys, come on, kiss Nana goodbye. It's best we go now before something else blows up. I'll call you as soon as I can." Jimmy knew Mom meant when she could talk without Dad present. Mom and the two boys went out and got into the police car. Dad didn't say anything, just started the car and it rolled down the short bit of hill and turned right on the highway. Looking back, Jimmy could see Gramp on the porch, stiff and seeming taller than he had in years.

CHAPTER 7

Jimmy seems to be developing a talent for eavesdropping, and some might say that my career as a reporter was just a logical follow-through. But I think I can say that this incident was abnormal. As a child, I wasn't too interested in adult affairs, and any curiosity I might have had was easily satisfied by asking Mom. It was rare for her to say that something wasn't my business. In the case of Gloria Peet's body — sorry, can't get out of that habit of thought, the body we thought to be Gloria Peet's — Jimmy's curiosity was surely natural, yet he did not contrive to overhear his father and grandfather fight. In fact, he sat on that toilet wishing he were just about anywhere else.

The mystery of the body was rather bloodless, like the body itself. It was a puzzle conveniently solved by the facts that someone was missing at the appropriate time, and that this someone had no living connections. Dehumanization of the victim was easy, even for those who had viewed the body, perhaps especially for them. Gloria Peet and her mummified remains became a curiosity, part of the folklore of Cobalt. I wonder if she, living in Toronto or somewhere, aged 31 in 1949, ever saw a news item about the body and its presumed identity. Was she already launched on her career as showgirl-cum-courtesan, already using one of a string of aliases? I'm certain one of the Toronto papers must have picked up the story, but I'm less sure that Gloria was a regular reader of anything except men's intentions.

Well, if this record is eventually going to find its way to Willy, I can see he might be disappointed at his marginal role in these stirring events. But why should a seven year old know what's going on? When I was five, half my firmament was ripped away by my father's departure for war. By the time I was seven, whole weeks would pass without me thinking of him. By the time he returned, when I was nine, he was practically a stranger. I'm sure that Willy, when he thought of that Sunday, would remember the dinghy skating across Lake Temiskaming, not that Nana was in tears when he came into the house or that we departed so quickly and guiltily. Adult tears are incomprehensible to someone who cries only out of immediate pain or frustration, and who knows why adults do something quickly or slowly anyway?

Jimmy's main emotion was embarrassment. His father had caused a scene, and no one hates a scene more than a young teenager, unless he is the cause of it, and then it is not, by definition, a scene. The odd thing is that my father, as he sat out in that car refusing to come back in, was also deeply embarrassed. He had schooled himself — I think, during the war — to a stoicism that was almost stolidity. He had curbed the temperament which had led him, as a teenager himself, into conflict with his father and eventually into leaving home. And now the temperament had reasserted itself, but for what? he had violated the policeman's code; he had allowed his personal feelings to creep (not the right word — flare?) into an investigation. Not only had he gained no new information, he had hopelessly muddled anything from that source.

Jimmy had not heard everything that had passed between Gramp and Dad, but he had heard enough that he should have known that the breach between the two was not going to heal easily or quickly, if ever. On the other hand, no one else in the car had the least idea that he had overheard anything. It was probably unfortunate that he had overheard the fight, for it made him conscious of the fact that the estrangement of Gramp and Dad was tied up with Aunt Evvy without giving him enough facts to judge anything on. Thus, like many teenagers among friends, he was feeling pushed into taking sides without any real information to go on. Right now, his father seemed to be the aggressor, and maybe that fit just too neatly into everything else that happens to adolescent boys in relation to their fathers.

Jimmy and Willy were in the back seat of the car during the silent trip from Haileybury to Cobalt. Dad's neck, the back of it, was red, not just sunburned, but suffused with red from within. Past his head, Jimmy could see his wristwatch on the arm holding the wheel. It was only four-thirty. The whole thing at the house had not taken more than fifteen or twenty minutes, and yet for Jimmy, the day had self-destructed, blown apart by waves of emotion riding words through a window.

The sun was still fairly high, but the hill going past the courthouse was steep and the sun shone for a few blocks directly into the windshield. Mom shielded her face. Willy said, "Aren't we eating at Nana's? and Jimmy shushed him. Mom was looking directly ahead at the road. Dad drove at a steady fifty miles per hour, except in North Cobalt where he slowed to thirty. Nothing more was said in the car.

When they got home, Mom said, "I'll get us some supper. You boys go upstairs and wash." Dad followed her into the kitchen, and Jimmy paused on the stairs looking at their backs. Mom was looking into the fridge.

"Look, Peg, you don't understand what was happening back there."

"Of course I don't understand, Pete. Understanding means having some facts to work with. I love you, and yes, I trust you, but I can't say I understand. There's something going on between you and your father that you won't tell me about, or at least you never have. And just this last two weeks it's gotten worse. And you're not telling me why. What's that phrase you use in the police reports? From information received. Well, Pete, from information received, I don't know a damned thing about what's going on."

"I just wanted to …"

"What, Pete, wanted to what?"

"See those letters he says he got from Evvy."

"Well?"

"He was just getting them, or maybe one of them, when we heard Willy come in and he shut the desk. Then he blew up at me."

"You're in uniform, Pete. Was that the kind of looking you were doing?"

"I don't know …" Then Dad turned and saw Jimmy on the stair. For a second, his face looked almost scared. Jimmy started up the stairs again, and only heard the last bit. "Maybe we can talk later. The kids. Jimmy was just listening."

"Yes, we should talk later, Pete. Me and your mother, we have a right." Jimmy heard no more. He followed Willy to the bathroom and caught him making his "handsome" face in the mirror. It consisted of eyes narrowed to slits and mouth drawn taut in an expression which might look like Roy Rogers, but which even Willy would admit didn't have the effect of the original.

Jimmy decided to tease. "Looks more like Trigger. Or maybe Dale Evans." The last was too much for Willy who threw his washcloth in Jimmy's face, and in a second they were tussling. Jimmy got on top, and used the washcloth to complete a vigorous scrubbing of Willy's face. Both of them were giggling when Mom appeared at the bathroom door.

"Great! Look at the water on the floor, and your clothes. Honestly, you two ... all three of you!" But she wasn't really mad or anything. "Get up and let's go downstairs. Cold ham and warm beans."

They ate, of course, in the kitchen. Mom had once said, sort of wistfully, that some day they might have a dining room. Probably ninety-five percent of the people in Cobalt ate in their kitchens. The only dining rooms Jimmy had ever seen were in Haileybury, and the one in Mrs. Ross' house two blocks over, one of Mom's reading friends.

Dad had changed from his uniform. "I put it on after I saw the accident site this morning. Old Man Sundstrom was out trying to catch that crazy cow of his in West Cobalt when he heard the crash, and went over to the highway to have look. Then he had to get to a phone, and Hadley's was the closest. I got there neck and neck with Hec Belanger, and together we got the guy out of the wreck. It looked like both legs were broken, and he was knocked out, of course. Anyway, Hec took him up to the Haileybury Hospital, and I got hold of Lucky Johnston to tow the wreck. It's a wonder the guy wasn't killed — he'd gone off the road straight into that rock. I had his registration and licence, but I thought I'd get into uniform before I went to talk to him in the hospital. That's when I saw your note."

"Is he going to be all right?" Mom asked.

"Sure. He was awake by the time I got up to Haileybury. Unhappy though. Seems he'd driven all night from Toronto, heading for Timmins. Just fell asleep at the wheel, dam fool. But as long as I was in Haileybury, I thought I'd go over to the house and ask ... and see if you guys were ready to come home."

The stove had been off all day, and Mom hadn't built a fire for just this meal. The beans had been warmed on the little electric hot plate, and while we were eating, she had a big kettle balanced on the thing. It was warm enough to wash the dishes, so she began the washing, and Willy the drying while Dad and Jimmy went out to replenish the wood box. Dad chopped, splitting the logs with clean, economical strokes, while Jimmy kept setting up the new piece to be split. Then they loaded up for the first of two trips to the big wood box in the kitchen. "Do a little kindling too, we're short." Jimmy got the hatchet and started worrying away at a piece of dry birch. Dad watched. Jimmy knew that Dad would just grab the big axe, gripping it up near the head and use it like a tackhammer on a piece of wood, the kindling flying away like toothpicks. The phone rang inside, and Dad stopped, looking over the fence while waiting to see if Mom got it. It was almost as if he were a hunting dog, pointing at a partridge.

"Pete, it's your mother. Something's happened." Dad ran for the kitchen door. Jimmy followed, kindling forgotten.

"...Where is he now, and where are you? ... OK, the hospital. Did the doctor say anything? ... Oh....oh, that, yes ... what else? ... Of course it's enough, Ma, I just meant ... Yes, we'll be there as soon as I can get hold of Jim and get a taxi... Yes, Ma, within an hour at most. I'm going to hang up now, so we can get moving. OK? Good. Let the sisters know, and they'll find you a place to rest. Bye, Ma." He hung up and immediately cranked for the operator. "Helen, could you locate Jim for me? I've got the duty, and my father's had something, maybe a stroke up in Haileybury. Tell Jim the car's in front of my place. Oh, and get me Ron's Taxi."

Mom said, "You go up, Pete. I'll say here with the kids."

"No, we'll all go. He's their grandfather. I'm not sure we can all see him, but Ma's going to need some distraction, someone to be with."

Three or four minutes later there was a honk outside.In that time, Dad had talked with Uncle Jim and Jimmy and Willy had changed into long pants and leather shoes. In the taxi, Dad sat up front with Ron Kelsey. "Hi Lil. Anything wrong? Helen said to move fast."

"It's OK, Ron, don't break any speed limits. We've got to go to the Haileybury Hospital — it's my father, a stroke or something. And don't do any bootlegging while you think I'm out of town. Jim's got the duty."

"Me bootleg? With the thousands I make in the cab business, do you think I'd descend to selling hooch? Two bucks to Haileybury, Lil, more if I have to wait to bring you back."

"No need. We'll get Roly from that end — a dollar seventy-five, I hear."

"Yeah, and a car that might just make the trip. Up to you, Lil." While the bargaining was going on, the taxi was almost through downtown, and heading up the hill on Lang Street. The sun was much lower now, and the shadows of the houses on the left were climbing up the houses on the other side of the street.

Everyone was silent. Jimmy was thinking about strokes. Harry's grandmother had had a stroke while Harry and Jimmy were in St. Pat's school. She had never come out of the hospital, just lay in a bed there for six weeks and then she died. But what had happened to her had never been clear. "Mom, what is a stroke?"

"Well, first of all, we're not sure yet whether that's what happened to Gramp. It could be something else. But I guess you could say a stroke is a sort of accident to the arteries and veins inside the brain. Some strokes come from something blocking the artery, and part of the brain can't get blood, so it dies. Others are a break in an artery or vein, and the blood spills out into the brain, but other parts are cut off again from the normal supply."

"Do you, um, die?"

"Sometimes, if it's big. Sometimes it means the person can't talk, or can't move parts of his body. Sometimes they recover pretty completely."

Jimmy saw that Dad was looking back at them. "I'm sorry, Dad. About Gramp, I mean."

"Sure, son. These things happen. He's almost seventy."

The taxi was through Hundred and Four and pulling up the hill and around the curve by the cemetery. In there, the French and the English — non-French, one should say, since they were a polyglot group that went to St, Patrick's — were buried right next to each other, their catholicity finally overcoming their language differences. Jimmy wondered why he got hung up on words like polyglot, and yet didn't know much about strokes. He prayed for a minute, promising God that he'd become a doctor and save all sorts of people if God would give Gramp a break now. Then the taxi was over the small rise and going past the Blue Top Cabins, the southern edge of North Cobalt. Ron glanced over at Dad, and kept the speed at fifty.

"Thirty here, Ron," growled Dad, and the taxi slowed.

"Geez, you're never off duty, are you Lil?"

"Sometimes I wish I were."

Soon they were past the old streetcar diner, one of the last relics of the streetcar line that had once linked the three towns, and entering the long curves, first right, then left that filled the gap between North Cobalt and Haileybury. The hospital was on this end of town, the French end as Gramp called it. It was the biggest building in town, three stories in a long rectangle along the crest of the hill overlooking Lake Temiskaming. Ron went down the street past the Emergency entrance, turned onto Georgina, then did a U turn to drop them at the front sidewalk. "Hope things are OK, Lil. I'd almost forgotten your old man lived here — never see him in Cobalt much, not like during the war."

"No, he doesn't come down there much. Thanks, Ron." The two dollars changed hands. Willy was fumbling with the door handle on his side, and Mom leaned over to help him. Jimmy got out the left side. Dad walked quickly up the walk with its two short sets of stairs, and held the door open for them. "You guys wait in that little room over there. There's some games and stuff for kids. Peg, let's see if we can find Ma."

Over an hour went by, and Jimmy tired of the dogeared comics available. There weren't any crime comics, and they were the most interesting, particularly as they were forbidden fruit. Mom said they should be outlawed, that they glorified a bunch of thugs. He had said "But you read Dick Tracy."

Her reply had been "You should be able to tell the difference between realism and fantasy by now." and that had stopped him cold. Now he looked at an issue of *The Phantom*, and wondered how come the Phantom wore that costume in the middle of Africa, and Tarzan never wore much of anything. Neither did Sheena, Queen of the Jungle. In fact, she wore so little, and that so clinging, that Jimmy had a fair, if exaggerated idea of female anatomy, in this case fantastic rather than realistic. No Sheena here either. Then a nun poked her head into the room.

"Jimmy and Willy Thorpe?"

"Yes, Sister." Jimmy had a nun as a teacher in Grades Four, Five and Six, and had learned deference the hard way. This nun had one of those faces that couldn't be dated; she might be twenty-five, she might be fifty-five. There was something about the wimple and the way it outlined the face, no hair visible, that made nuns look so … in control.

"Come along. You can see your grandfather for a minute now."

Gramp was lying in a bed on the second floor. A tank of oxygen stood beside the bed, and a tube went to a mask over his face. His hair looked like it had been wet and dried in clumps, going in different directions on the pillow. His chest rose and fell slowly with a rhythmic hiss from the mask. A tube went from his left arm up to a bag of something dark. His hands looked white and limp. There was a sob in the room, and Jimmy realized that Willy was crying. He pulled him over and put his arm around his small shoulders.

Dad was at the foot of the bed, staring at Gramp. Mom was sitting beside Nana with her arm around her shoulders, and Jimmy could hear her speaking softly, "Catherine, all we can do is wait. He's got a strong constitution, you heard the doctor say that, and there may be some improvement by tomorrow. Don't worry, we'll stay with you."

"Just you, Peggy."

"What?"

"I don't think Pete should stay at the house tonight. I'm not sure I want him there."

"But Catherine, you don't think ..."

"That he caused this? In a way I do, I guess. After you left, I don't think I've ever seen him so angry, not since Pete left home way back. Oh, nobody was angry at him marrying you, Peggy, Lord knows you're the best part of Pete's life, but he was so, well. headstrong when he was a kid, and it seemed nothing Peter could do would make him, um, behave."

Jimmy watched the subject of this conversation. He held Willy tight to his side. and saw Mom doing the same with Nana, but there, one at the foot of the bed and the other lying along it were two men forever separate.

CHAPTER 8

One thing about the "replay" quality of these memories is the renewal of my admiration for my mother. It's not that her temperament was necessarily placid; it's more that she had long ago internalized the lesson of the limits of effect, that one could wish that things were another way, but in the long run, we have to accept that our effect on our circumstances is not going to be great. Because ninety percent of our circumstances consists of other people, and because she knew that you can't really change other people, it followed that you didn't raise a fuss.

Or am I making too much of this, do I see her in a rosy glow because I never fully separated from her, never extended my rebellion in her direction? I was going to move into that period of complete self-reference we call adolescence, and when she died (six and a half years after the summer I've been remembering), I was barely twenty, never to know her through adult eyes. My eyes are watering as I write this, remembering her explanation of strokes in the taxi, for she was to die before forty of a massive stroke, the bursting of an aneurism in the brain. Since that death, I have felt a gap in my life, one that only barely seems filled with my own family. Lest Ken or Laura ever read this, let me hasten to say that they and their mother, my own Dee, are as dear to me as my imagination can conceive. It's just that, no matter how happy my family has made me, and that happiness was, on certain levels, complete, there is still a part of me that misses Mom and knows she can never be replaced within me.

While I remember Nana making that statement about Dad, I have never thought that she was rejecting him, or even fully blaming him. Jimmy at the time put it down to her being upset and afraid, and I think he was right — I almost said "I was right", for I'm feeling closer to my young protagonist, my younger self. In any event, I do remember (in the conventional call-it-to-mind-now sense) that we, Willy and I, returned to Cobalt with Dad that night, and Mom stayed with Nana. Dad was on day duty that week, and even arranged with a vacationing OPP constable to cover for a couple of days, so we spent a lot of time in Haileybury. Willy was a focus that allowed my grandmother to feel normal while my grandfather's body fought to survive, and, maybe, bring his mind back to consciousness.

In the end, of course, he never fully recovered. He did go home from the hospital after three weeks, having been seen by a neurologist from Toronto (who actually flew up). Gramp was conscious long before the three weeks were up, but he couldn't speak, and his whole right side was paralyzed. He could think, though, and he was pretty frustrated by the failure of his efforts to be understood. The first month he was home, they had a nurse come in — two at first, day and night, but then one — to help him bathe, shave, eat, dress. The process almost drove him crazy, and he learned pretty quickly how to get in and out of the wheelchair with the help of some grab bars. If Nana laid out his clothes in a particular way, he could even dress himself, though she would handle the buttons. No Velcro in those days. He had a device installed on the stairs onto which he would run his wheelchair (it was one of the first battery powered chairs in Northern Ontario), and clamp it down, then work the control to go up or down the stairs.

I remember that I rode it upstairs one day when he was in his study. His moan of inarticulate rage was clear to all within the house when he came to the bottom of the stairs. But that was much later.

Mom spent most of the last week of August and the first week of September up in Haileybury, helping Nana. She had a natural tact which let her hang back from tasks Nana was ready to take on, but to provide unobtrusive help when needed. Finally it was clear that with the nurses plus a daily "househelper", a diminutive French lady who whirled through tasks with energy and speed that would do credit to a bantam boxer, Nana would get along very well. This was good, because we were moving.

Dad had received an offer from the Wright-Hargreaves, a gold mine in Kirkland Lake, of a job as head of security. At the time, the offer seemed to me to have come out of the blue, but I grew to suspect that he had let his availability be known, and between his pre-war friends and his army buddies, all was arranged. The Town of Cobalt tried counter-offers, but their only effect was to alert Uncle Jim to the amount the town was actually prepared to pay for policing. He too let his availability be known, and it was he who reaped the largesse from the town coffers. For Dad it was obviously more than an economic decision: he wanted out, out of police work, out of the Tri-Town. The money was much better than our family was used to, and shortly after the move, Dad actually bought his first car, a used Hudson.

For me and Willy, the move was high adventure. Kirkland Lake was, at that time, five or six times the size of Cobalt, and qualified as a BIG town, one that boasted three movie theatres and about six restaurants, only two of which were Chinese. We never wondered particularly whether we would miss Cobalt (though I did suffer from homesickness in some ways after the move), and both of us knew, though we never said it aloud, that it would be a relief to be farther away from Gramp. His misery was palpable, a gloom that filled the big house, punctuated by outbursts of wordless but not voiceless anger.

Dad had offered the town a months's notice, but they were sure they could keep him, and didn't look for a replacement until the last week, when they had to appeal to the OPP. They grudgingly assigned a young officer to Cobalt for a few months, and billed the town twice Dad's salary. We were to move on Monday, October 3rd, so my last day at Cobalt High School was Friday. Dad, Mom and Willy would go up by train, but I had the privilege of riding in the moving van, in a little space, top rear, nestled in a tangle of furniture. On Wednesday, I would register at Kirkland Lake Collegiate and Vocational Institute, K.L.C.V.I., a school of almost a thousand students, five times the size of Cobalt High. That scared me.

But to pull back for a moment: I'm starting to get the hang of this memory sweeping, and I know that this memoir, or whatever it is, has to deal with my last Saturday in Cobalt. So, I'll turn things over to Jimmy again. I'm sure he'll oblige me with a full picture of what happened that day. How soon, I'm less sure, for these days it sometimes takes a week, even more, for the memory to start.

"OK, Jimmy. I know Kirkland Lake has three theatres. I know that one of them runs movies continuously every day from one o'clock. All of us know about the restaurants and K.L.C.V.S. Can you lay off for a while?" Harry was sounding really exasperated.

"I"

"You what?"

"K.L.C.V.I. not K.L.C.V.S. It's an Institute, not a School."

"Jimmy, you're going to drive me nuts. I guess I'm going to miss you, but not right away. Look, my mother wanted me to get home early for lunch. My aunt is coming over. I'll see you before you go, right?"

"Right. I've got a couple of things to do. See you, Harry." They had been batting an old tennis ball in the vacant lot beside the Finn Hall. Jimmy sat on a rock and watched Harry disappear down Nickel Street. All week he had been checking things off mentally: the last time doing this, the last time going in the old school, the last time … Harry was right about him being boring,but the talking was coming from excitement. Last week, Dad had borrowed Nana's car —well, it was Gramp's car, but it looked like he would never drive it again, and Jimmy was pretty sure Nana didn't tell Gramp who was borrowing it — and they all drove up to Kirkland Lake, about 70 miles. They were going to live in a house right on the mine property, and Mom wanted to get some measurements.

The house was OK, but Jimmy was more interested in exploring the town, so he took Willy, and they walked for hours, going out as far as the Lakeshore Mine. There was the big lodge built by Harry Oakes, Sir Harry Oakes, who had staked the Lakeshore and run the big mine for many years until he was murdered down in the Caribbean during the war. Stretching east from the Lakeshore was the "Three Miles of Gold" that had made prospectors rich in the short term and stockbrokers in Toronto richer for longer. It ran all the way to the Sylvanite and the Wright-Hargreaves.

The Lakeshore Mine was on the shore of what used to be a lake, but now was a desolate slime. With rudimentary equipment and lots of dynamite, men had forced their way over a mile down into the earth, and had carved out huge caverns on all sides. Every bit of rock had been hauled up to the surface, where some ("waste") was dumped in mountainous piles, and the rest ("ore") was ground to a fine powder in monstrous mills, mixed with water and chemicals, run over vibrating tilted tables, filtered and washed until it yielded up the gold within it to be smelted, poured into bars, and shipped in tightly guarded railway cars to the south. The liquid remaining was known as tailings, or slimes, and it was poured out to fill what used to be the lake which gave the town its name. It spilled over the former shores to kill a forest as well, hundreds of dead trunks, blackened in death and sprouting obscenely coloured fungi. To Jimmy and Willy, it looked perfectly normal. This was a mining town.

The men whose muscles had torn this from the earth were not insensitive to beauty, but they defined it in terms of their homelands, Italy, Galicia, Croatia, Poland,. The seemingly endless forest of the Canadian Shield was simply "bush" and there was so much of it that covering a few square miles with a grey semi-liquid, semi-poisonous puddle didn't strike them as wrong. What was wrong was the division of the spoils. A bitter strike was only a couple of years in the past, a strike in which the owners had held solid and broken the power of the union, then assisted another union, an American one, to wipe out the membership of the militant one. Naturally, the strikers had been called communists, and indeed many admired Tim Buck and had not given up the wartime admiration of Uncle Joe Stalin.

As Jimmy and Willy made their way back to the Wright-Hargreaves property and their parents, they knew nothing of this. Nor did they know that their father, in his new high-paying job, was lining up with the owners. This sort of thing wasn't important to Willy, and Jimmy was still reading *Time* and imbibing its religion. More exciting was the news that real professional wrestling was coming to the Teck Arena, with Gorgeous George, Whipper Billy Watson and more. And the show would be there in three weeks, when they would be living just three blocks away!

Now, as Jimmy counted the hours till the move, one thing nagged at him. Harry was out of sight. Jimmy got up decisively and went down the street, pausing to lean his bat against the steps of his house, but carrying on to where the steps went down to the public school. He ducked to one side and felt under the first step, his fingers digging down into the cold earth. He brought up several handfuls of dirt, sifting each through his hands, examining each pebble. Then he had it, the ring with the purple stone. He clambered back onto the steps, looked at it, and slipped it into his pocket.

Willy was up in Haileybury with Nana. Mom was packing in the house, and had shooed him out two hours ago. He looked up the street at his house and considered asking for permission. But the explanation would be impossible, he'd have to lie. If he just went, she'd never need to know. It would be handy to have his bike, but it was already in with a tangle of things on the porch, waiting for the movers.

He went down the forty-five steps in the barely controlled fall he had learned in the eight years of going down them, then through the rock cut by the school, and down the short hill to the railway tracks. The tracks were the shortest way to the north end of town, and going that way saved a lot of up and down, particularly the Lang Street hill. He adjusted his pace to take two ties at a time, breaking the monotony occasionally by walking along the shiny top of a rail. Past the LaRose Mine, site of the first silver find in Cobalt and still operating forty-six years later. Past the Right-of-Way Mine, long boarded up. Finally he was at the overpass, where the highway went over the tracks. He clambered up the steep bank, and looked hopefully toward the town for a northbound car.

Two cars passed him, and the third stopped. It was Mr. Hudson, who lived three doors south of Gramp and Nana. "Hi there, Jimmy. Going up to Haileybury for a visit? Hop in." Jimmy had to explain that he wasn't going all the way to Haileybury, just to this side of North Cobalt. "What are you doin' there, out in the middle of nowhere?"

"Visiting the cemetery. I just wanted to say a little prayer at, um, Mrs. Slater's grave." If Mr. Hudson was curious why Jimmy Thorpe wanted to visit the grave of an old woman who was no kin, and who had died two years ago, he didn't show it. It was only a mile and a half, and he dropped Jimmy at the entrance road. The wrought iron gates were closed with a simple catch. Jimmy carefully fastened them behind him.

The grave was easy to find because the grass hadn't had time to cover it completely, and the mound was higher than most of the graves. A simple rounded piece of limestone said "Gloria Peet

1918-1932. Rest in Peace". Jimmy felt the ring in his pocket, turning it again and again, feeling the sharpness of the purple stone. This would bring the whole thing to a close. He shuddered. Down there under the earth was a pine box with the mummy he had found seven weeks earlier, and he had the ring she had worn to her earlier, colder grave. Perhaps the body missed the ring somehow, was calling for it, might even come out of the grave ... Mom said the horror comics were almost as bad as the crime comics, and maybe she was right.

He crouched at the small headstone and quickly tucked the ring into the earth right along the stone, directly below the "in" of "Rest in Peace". He stood and stared at the spot. The ring wasn't visible. He turned slowly around. No one had seen him. The poplars were turning yellow and a cold breeze brought air from Hudson Bay. Already there was frost some mornings. The hottest summer since 1939 was finally finished.

When he got back to the highway, he started to cross it so he could walk and hitch-hike south. Then he decided to hitch-hike both ways; if he got a ride north to Haileybury, he could ride home with Willy and nana. If he got a ride south, it made no difference. He felt totally free, ready to go in any direction fate decreed. What if someone said, "HI, kid, I'm heading up to Kirkland Lake"? He could just go and phone back and say he'd see everyone Monday night. Dreamer. Besides, he was looking forward to his little cocoon in the moving van.

As it turned out, the first vehicle was a half-ton heading north. They stopped, an old farmer and his wife, and Jimmy hopped into the box. "Where you going, son?'

"Haileybury."

"We're going out the West Road from there, so we'll drop you at the top of the hill, OK?"

"Sure. Thanks a lot."

Rather than follow the highway through town, Jimmy followed streets in a zigzag pattern, a long block north, a short one downhill to the east, another long one to the north, and so on, till he emerged a block from Gramp's house. Nana was surprised to see him. "I've just been on the phone to your mother. You're all going to eat here tonight, and she was going to phone me when you showed up, so I could pick you all up."

"Isn't Willy here?"

"Of course he is. I meant you and your Mom and Dad."

Dad was coming to dinner. Jimmy didn't think he'd been in this house since he helped Gramp home from the hospital, and on that occasion there had been an atmosphere of tension and, maybe the word was too strong, but ... hatred? "Oh, I just thought I'd catch the bus and see you." Nana would get nervous if he told her about hitch-hiking, so the white lie was just to spare her nerves.

"Now I'll just phone her that you're here, and drive down to pick up the two of them. You can take care of anything your grandfather needs?" Nana never said "eh". Mom said it was because she was from Pennsylvania.

"Sure, Nana." Willy decided to go with her. Jimmy went into the living room. The sight of Gramp reminded him of a poem they'd taken last year, "The Dying Eagle", something about the fierceness left in the eyes after the strength of the body had gone. Gramps right hand lay in his lap like a dead bird, fingers half curled and pointing up. His right foot was twisted slightly, having moved when Gramp had shifted the side of his body he could still move in the chair. Jimmy crossed to him and straightened the foot. A half smile came on Gramp's face — literally a half smile, the left side only, with the right side of his mouth hanging slack, some saliva dripping from the corner. Jimmy grabbed a Kleenex and wiped the old man's face. Gramp grunted, an "Unhhh" sound which Jimmy took to mean thank you.

Then Nana and Willy passed through the living room, waved, and went out to the porch and the front steps. Gramp's eye followed them. Soon the sound of the engine starting seemed to galvanize him; he grunted and waved his left hand at Jimmy, then used the small joystick to start the chair towards his study. Jimmy followed him into the room and over to the desk. Gramp grabbed the handle of a desk drawer on the right, a deep drawer, but he had no leverage, and the hand was pulling at a difficult angle. The drawer moved half an inch, then stopped. Gramp grabbed his control again, and backed away from the desk, motioning to Jimmy.

Jimmy pulled on the drawer, which seemed stuck until suddenly it opened with a screech of wood on wood. The drawer was stuffed with folders. Jimmy looked at Gramp, wondering which one he wanted. "Do you want a file out, Gramp?"

The head wobbled from side to side, and the left hand cut across his body. No. Then Gramp found the pencil dangling from the left arm of the wheelchair, gripped it in his fist, and began to print awkwardly on the little pad attached to the arm of the chair. Straight stroke by straight stroke, he formed "ALL". Jimmy leaned over to start pulling out the files, but was stopped by a grunt from Gramp. The old man was printing again. First there was an arrow pointing downwards, then, slowly and laboriously, the word "BASEMENT".

"OK, Gramp, I'll take these to the basement. All right if I put them in a box down there?"

The wobble of the head was now up and down, so Jimmy began pulling the files out and piling them on the desk. When they were all in one pile, he lifted it and started for the basement. He had to put the pile down to get the light switch at the top of the stairs, but he got them down to the gloomy cavern, located a wooden butter box (perhaps intended for kindling before the automatic oil furnace went in), slid the files into it, and lifted it to a high shelf. The white wood of the butter box stood out against the dark concrete. Then he went up to the main floor to announce the completion of the mission.

Twenty minutes later, the car arrived back from Cobalt. Jimmy watched Dad and Gramp. Dad's eyes never seemed to go near the old man, while Gramp's eyes followed the big man compulsively. Was it fear or anger? It was no pleasant emotion, Jimmy was sure of that. Nana had cooked a stew, and Mom fed Gramp carefully cut up stew by spoon, patiently as with a baby. He chewed, but if the food wandered over to the right side of his mouth, it was obvious he lost control of it. His eyes were fixed on Dad throughout dinner.

After supper, they all sat in the living room for half an hour. Nana said they should stay to listen to Lux Radio Theatre. How Green was My Valley was on that night. Dad threw a desperate look at Mom, who said no, they had an early morning coming to get to early mass and finish packing, but we'd stay for an hour to get the dishes done and relax a little. Gramp started up his chair and headed for the stairs, and they heard the whine of the stair elevator motor. Nana followed him to help him into bed.

"He's sleeping twelve hours at a stretch now," she said as she left the room. Mom signalled to Jimmy and Willy and they followed her into the kitchen. Soon there was a pile of suds in the big double sink, Mom up to her elbows in it, and the two boys in an intricate gavotte, swooping in to get a dish out of the drainer, circling out again to avoid collision with the other dryer. Jimmy was putting a pot into the big cupboard at the end of the kitchen when he heard squeal of wood on wood. After a moment's thought, he slipped out to the living room. His Dad was still sitting in the small (for him) armchair.

Nana came downstairs just as they were finishing, and protested that they shouldn't have done the dishes. But Jimmy thought she looked exhausted, five years older than she had looked two months before. Her protests when Dad called for a taxi to go home were feeble.

CHAPTER 9

I suppose that last weekend in Cobalt was the first intimation I had that my allegiance was going to shift, the first faint suspicion that my father was not all-wise and all-knowing. All kids have to go through this as a necessary part of growing up, and it is one of the painful parts of being a teenager (and, from the other side, of having a teenager around) that we humans don't seem to be able to do these things smoothly. If Father is imperfect, the adolescent seems duty bound to magnify the imperfections, to demonize the parent, until some sort of nadir of adolescence is reached, and the teenager can begin to grow out of it and gain a new, adult respect for Dad. It's the source of the old joke: "When I was sixteen, I realized that my father was an incompetent fool. When I came back at twenty-one, I was amazed to see how much the old man had learned in five short years."

In my case, the initial part of this process was hastened by the conflict between Gramp and Dad. Jimmy didn't necessarily realize, at least not consciously, how this conflict was tied up with the body in the mine, or even that its sources were back somewhere in Dad's childhood. He just saw Dad acting, he thought, irrationally. And the effect on Gramp was the stroke. Nothing is quite as keen as a teenager's sense of injustice, and Jimmy was ready to take the side of Gramp, the underdog.

I don't know to this day if Dad ever confided to Mom exactly what was driving him. She never spoke about it to Jimmy (as I think of myself up to the beginning of 1950, when I turned fourteen) or to Jim (as I was from then until 1956, the year of her death). Once, when Willy, about six months after we moved to Kirkland Lake, burst out with "Remember that body that Jimmy found?", Mom silenced him with one look. And so Dad's refusal to talk about it engendered a silence on the topic through the whole family. And it is curious how once an island of non-communication appears in a sea of free communication, it can grow into an archipelago or a continent inhabited with things we don't talk about.

I wonder if Willy, when he reads this, will notice that the memories are changing somewhat. The me who is writing it down seems more able to intrude upon the past. For example, I look at what I wrote about the landscape and the labour strife in Kirkland Lake, and I know it had nothing to do with Jimmy's reaction to the sights, but is instead the reporter in me sticking a little editorial into a story, something we objective types are not supposed to do unless we do it so skilfully that no one notices. This is probably because I am growing to feel some identity with the emerging Jim, the new Russian doll growing to enclose the child Jimmy. "Shades of the prison house begin to close upon the growing boy." I wonder if that's what Wordsworth meant, that the choices we make while growing, the options we choose, necessarily close other choices off and restrict our freedom. The very process of becoming shuts down much of our potential, and Jim, while he might contain Jimmy, has lost some of the spontaneity of his younger self. Maybe we are most free when youngest, most dependent on our parents. As we get older, we face the tyranny of our peers, or the tyranny of our fears about what our peers <u>might</u> think, and this is every bit as restrictive as parental rule.

The external view of our family changed in Kirkland Lake, and this had its effect on Jim as well as on the areas of non-communication within the house. In Cobalt, Dad had represented, along with Uncle Jim, the whole majesty of the law, present, immediate, and imposing in ways that even the judge, up in the District Town of Haileybury, couldn't match. Jimmy, whether he knew it or not, basked in reflected glory. In Kirkland Lake, earning almost twice as much money, Dad seemed socially shrivelled. He was a company cop, and his writ did not run outside the Wright-Hargreaves property. He was the natural enemy of some of the miners whose sons Jim knew at school. Dad had as his job the prevention of high grading and the observation of certain "Red" unionists, men management felt were not fully converted from the Mine Mill and Smelter Workers' ideology to the more compliant Steelworkers' frame of mind. Not that Jim found himself in tough conflicts because of this, for most teenagers in Kirkland Lake did not dwell on the union battles of a few years before, but there was an undercurrent, and the social antennae of teenagers are very sensitive to disapproval.

I believe that Kirkland Lake was run in those days by Reeve Ann Shipley, who was reelected often enough that Jim thought "Reeve" was her first name, not the title of a township council chair. She was a Liberal, and appeared on a platform one day with the Governor General, Earl Alexander of Tunis, a handsome, top-drawer Brit, and W.L. Mackenzie King, Prime Minister, squat, decidedly unhandsome, and with no sense of being top-drawer. Jim listened to the speeches and decided that politics was dull. He did, however, take up debating. He was much too small for football, the legitimate route to social success in K.L.C.V.I., and debating suited his growing chutzpah. And he began to work on the school newspaper, writing some things, editing others, and working a hand mimeograph to crank out a thousand copies of a twenty page newspaper. Maybe I owe my reputation as a two-fisted journalist to that exercise, because he had to switch hands on the mimeograph machine or lose his right arm.

Then there was sex. Curiosity began to turn into obsession. One girl in particular seemed to get a lot of pleasure out of enticing, then repulsing, a fourteen year old boy who was smaller than the sixteen year olds around him. She had an adult figure and techniques of flirtation which thoroughly confused him. In some desperation, he attempted to act out some of his fantasies with a Grade Nine girl, and her panicky reaction was terrifying to him. Confusion reigned.

There was still no TV in Northern Ontario at this point, but the ethos of the Donna Reed show and Leave it to Beaver was there. A boy in sexual awakening was supposed to seek the advice of his father or his spiritual advisor. Jim did blurt out something about his sexual longings to the priest in the confessional, only to be met with an inquisition that was even more frightening. And somehow, he couldn't talk to Dad about it. To Mom, he wouldn't. Formal sex education was limited to one cryptic talk by the Phys Ed teacher about turning "excess energy" to sports., and some films on VD that were shown to the cadet corps to wide mystification (though no one would admit to being mystified). The worst thing about puberty was its loneliness. The other boys in his class were past it, but he could never admit to them his sense of newness.

But these are universal experiences. The specific in Jim's case was that his father was diminished in his eyes, and that diminution was tempting him towards contempt. Somehow, sympathy for Gramp (which was considerably easier to keep up at a distance of 70 miles) seemed to prohibit any sympathy for Dad.

Dad, I think, was not happy that year. Looking back, I can see that he was a good policeman, that his misstep with Gramp was an exception, an isolated incident. In Kirkland Lake, in his early thirties, he probably had that feeling of having missed his calling, of moving into a dead end. However much it paid right now, the mining industry, at least gold, was not healthy in Northern Ontario in the fifties, with the price fixed at thirty-two dollars an ounce. Postwar prosperity in Canada did not extend to gold-mining towns. There was also the fact that Dad had worked underground in the thirties, and was in the ranks during the war, and being an agent of the privileged class did not sit lightly with him. Anyway, unhappiness made him even less communicative and less sympathetic with a teenage son who was covering insecurity with a smokescreen of bravado. Dad began spending more time in the Legion. He never got drunk, but his silences grew.

I look at that word "silence" that I just wrote. At this moment, the day before Labour Day, the end of a soft Vancouver Island summer, I ask myself what I have said and to whom this past week. "Hello" or "Good Morning" on a walk doesn't count. Nothing in the past six days.

However, the fact that circumstances brought silence on Dad then and me now is not relevant to Jim's situation back in 1950. This was a few years before rock and roll began to provide refuge, escape, and a sense of generational separation. James Dean was not rebelling without cause yet, Elvis was still in the future, hair length merely marked your gender. There was no clear path of rebellion except shaving the curfew, skimping the chores, and just generally being miserable. Jim did what he could.

Things almost, but not quite, came to a head in the early summer, on a visit to Haileybury.

Haileybury 1950

They travelled down to Haileybury on Thursday, June 15th, the day after Jim's Latin exam. He was still burning about that. As usual, his marks had stayed in the upper half of the class, though his extra-curricular activities had cut into them considerably. But he thought he had plenty of margin to be exempted from examinations, as usual. Latin had tripped him up.

All through the year, Jim had been faking it a bit in Latin. He didn't really like the subject because it was so cut and dried, no room for improvisation. He had a good memory, so the use of cribs made translations into English easy. Going the other way required not only memory for the vocabulary, but a meticulous habit of construction, the strict application of grammatical rules, and an interest in the language which he did not possess. Fortunately, he thought, there was a way out. The Latin teacher, a tall cadaverous man named Forrester, was keen on getting the class to really appreciate, as he put it, "the grandeur that was Rome". He offered bonus marks to students who were willing to stand up in front of the class and expound on some points of Roman culture, mythology, military organization, art — anything Roman. This was right up Jim's alley. He actually found the Romans very interesting, however boring their language might have been. It was easy to work up a new topic for exposition practically weekly, and he became Mr. Forrester's apostle to the Gentiles. He was dismayed at the beginning of June when Mr. Forrester kept him at the end of class.

"Jim, you've got a good mark in this class, do you know that?

Jim had it calculated to an exact 81. "Yes, sir, I've really enjoyed the class."

"I know, Jim. And you've added quite a bit to it with your talks on the Romans. It's been good having you in the class with all that enthusiasm."

"Thank you, sir."

"But, unfortunately, I have the feeling that you haven't learned as much Latin as you should. Not just a feeling. It is confirmed by your notebook and your test results. Would you agree?"

Trapped. "Um, I guess it's not my best subject, but I do try."

"I suspect that if you tried really hard, we could be having this conversation in Latin. Jim, I'm afraid you will have to write the final examination. I can't really exempt you, knowing that your work in the language itself doesn't merit the marks you've been getting. I'm sorry if you've developed false hopes." Mr. Forrester was a gentleman, and Jim hated him at that moment.

He developed what was probably the most elaborate cheat-sheet ever smuggled into an exam. All the conjugations and declensions were written on two sides of a single sheet of paper, in pencil so fine and letters so small that he would probably have to bring it within a foot of his face to read it. In the first rustle of examination papers being handed out, he got the sheet out of his pocket and unfolded in the cavity of the desk. He looked up. Mr. Forrester was looking at him unblinkingly. When the question paper arrived, he reviewed it quickly. Yes, he knew the sight passage by heart. And he realized with some surprise that he could handle most of the sentences to be translated into Latin. The preparation of that cheat-sheet was the most work he'd done all year in Latin, and it had prepared him as well as any other method of study. The sheet itself was irrelevant. He pulled out a handkerchief, noisily blew his nose, and with his other hand got the cheat-sheet out of the desk, crumpled it with the handkerchief and stuffed both into his pocket. Mr. Forrester was staring at him again, and he blushed. For the rest of the two hours, he feared a body search, but nothing happened.

Now, in the car going past Englehart, he was full of resentment. Forrester probably suspected him of cheating, but he never would have planned to, except for the fact that Forrester had forced him to write the exam. Even the knowledge that his inadvertent studying had allowed him to pass the exam easily made him angry, as if he had been tricked into the extra work. And there was no one to share his sense of injustice with; he could never even hint of it to Willy, Mom would have found it shameful on one level and hilarious on another, and Dad … Well, Dad would look at him with distaste and turn away.

The week of their planned visit coincided with the second week of Gramp's stay at a rehabilitation unit of Sunnybrook Hospital in Toronto. Sunnybrook was a veterans' hospital, and technically, Gramp would not have been eligible for treatment there, but it had the best rehab program in Canada for head injuries. His neurologist had pulled strings and gotten him into the program in the hopes of restoring some speech and maybe better functioning of some involuntary muscles, bowel and bladder control, and circulation in his right arm. Dad had not seen Gramp all year, and both seemed determined to keep it that way. As soon as Gramp was in the hospital in Toronto, Dad was willing to visit Haileybury.

That night, the three adults talked into the night. Jim, who had shed any scruples he might have had about eavesdropping, caught the gist of the conversation. Nana was getting more and more tired of dealing with an invalid's needs night and day. They had tried more nurses, but Gramp was quite unreasonable in his objections to every one, If there wasn't a change, Nana felt she was heading for a breakdown. "Pete, you wouldn't believe how exhausted I feel at the end of a day, and I have no assurance of much rest at night. We might find a nursing home somewhere, but I'm afraid it would kill him."

Mom fielded the unspoken request. "You'd like us to come and help, Catherine?"

"Yes, I would, but …"

"But Pete and Pa would just rub each other raw, right? Pete, I think you should tell your mother your plan."

"They're not full plans yet, Peg. OK, OK. Ma, I've had an offer from the OPP. They're looking for men with small town policing experience who are willing to go to Police College for a year and then enter the force. There's financial assistance. The only problem is that if I leave the mine job, we're out of the mine house, and , well …"

"Catherine, what he's trying to say is that there's not enough money. But if you need help, and you wouldn't mind me and the boys moving in for a year, then say so."

Jim couldn't hear much after that, but it sounded like Nana was crying and hugging Mom. Then they talked about Gramp's condition, which hadn't changed much as far as Jim could judge. He slipped back to bed. Dad was going to be away at the Police College down south somewhere. That would make Jim the man of the house, in a way — a very academic point, given Mom's personality. But Dad being gone would be good in some ways, less of that silent grumpy disapproval, no more curt orders to get on with a chore he'd been putting off for a bit. As for Gramp, Jim felt a sense of his own nobility in staying here to help the old man. And Nana would be so grateful to him. He guessed he'd go to Haileybury High School for Grade Twelve. It would be kind of small after the busy atmosphere of K.L.C.V.I., but he'd be able to show the guys here a thing or two. And he would be away from the tormenting daily presence of Rochelle.

In the morning it was made official in a formal family conference in the living room. Jim assumed his passive expression, not quite bored, but able to take any news in his stride. When his turn to express his opinion came, he had a neat little speech ready about the need for a family to help out in any way possible. Mom looked at him curiously, but Willy was quite impressed. Dad seemed relieved that there was no opposition, no talk about having to leave a circle of friends so painfully won. "All right, it's settled. I'll talk with Inspector Hanson on the phone today about the Police College, and I'll give notice to the mine. Jim, you'll be at cadet camp during our move. We'll probably make a couple of trips down, and Willy can stay here after the first one. Moving date will be about August 1st — is that OK with you, Ma?"

"When does the Police College start?"

"The fifteenth. But don't worry, I'll only be here a couple of days, and I'll stay out of Pa's way. He'll be glad Peg's here, and the boys. It'll work."

"Of course it will." She turned to Mom. "Peg, you've saved my life. You are more than a daughter."

Mom actually blushed, and mumbled something. The family conference broke up, and Jim and Willy headed down to the dinghy. "Life jackets, boys." Dad was in a good mood.

When they came back, having sailed about a hundred yards and rowed almost a mile, the car was gone. "Dad's gone down to Cobalt to talk with Uncle Jim about our plans. I'm glad he's doing this. Small town police forces are on the way out. Soon OPP detachments will be doing it all, and he might as well get in on the start of the trend." She was really happy, they could see the glow. "We'll be fine here in Haileybury. You boys will help to keep Gramp cheerful, I know. And you can each have your own room."

Two hours later, Dad came back, all cheerfulness gone. "Young man, I want to talk with you. In the study." Jim followed him into the study, mentally reviewing the last few weeks. Why the anger? Dad went to the desk, pulling a small straight-backed chair to one side of it and settling himself in Gramp's now unused swivel chair. "Sit down."

Jim sat in the small chair. There was silence that seemed to go on for minutes. Maybe Dad was expecting him to break down and confess something. Could Mr. Forrester have phoned him in Cobalt? Silently, they stared at each other. Then Dad shifted in his chair, and pulled some tissue paper from his pocket. He put it on the desk blotter and opened it. There was the ring with the purple stone. "Do you recognize this?"

"No, should I?" Defiance wasn't quite the right thing, but habit was strong.

"Maybe. It's an amethyst ring. It was found in a peculiar place this spring."

"So?"

A huge fist slammed down on the desk, and the ring jumped an inch into the air. "Don't you be bloody insolent with me, you young pup! It was found in the graveyard the other side of North Cobalt. On the grave of that girl you found last summer. Gloria Peet, or so everybody thinks."

"What do you want me to say?"

Dad sank back, suddenly looking tired. "The truth, Jim. The truth. This ring got there somehow. If the ring was connected with that body, there's darned few people who could have gotten it to the grave. It's evidence, that's what it is. Maybe evidence of who that girl was, and who killed her."

"I've never seen it before." His mind had circled around and knew that the lie was unassailable. His father couldn't prove anything.

"Did you ever visit that graveyard after you found the body?"

Quick calculation: Mr. Hudson had dropped him off there, and that could come out. "Yes, I did. The last weekend we were in Cobalt. I just wanted to ..."

"See the grave?"

"Yes. Mr. Hudson gave me a lift there, and I told him I was visiting another grave, To pray."

"That was one lie, Jim. Have you stopped lying?"

"Yes, sir." Defiance wasn't going to work. "I really never saw that ring."

His father leaned back again. "This is an amethyst, Jim, a birthstone. Do you know what month it's for?"

"No, sir. If it **was** Gloria Peet's birthstone, maybe someone who knew her ..."

"Gloria Peet was born in July. Her stone would be ruby. People say she wore several rings, but none of them had gemstones. Cameos, friendship rings, that sort of thing. Amethyst is for February, Jim. Know anybody born in February?"

"Hey, I wasn't even born when Gloria Peet got killed."

"Nobody's accusing you of anything, Jim. Except maybe taking a ring. Not stealing, I don't mean that. Maybe the ring fell from that hand. It was a left hand, wasn't it?"

"I ... I don't remember."

"Visualize it, Jim. After most of the ice got knocked off. While your father, the diligent cop, was down in that mine getting the rest of the body. The rest of the ice would have melted, right. Maybe the ring fell off — looks like it might fit the little finger of a fourteen or fifteen year old girl. It would be natural to pick it up, right?"

"I don't know, how could I know ..."

"it would be natural. And then later, you'd feel a little guilty. Not about evidence, cause I don't think you thought of it as evidence. But about taking something from a corpse. And it would be natural to want to return it to the grave of that girl, right?"

Time to take a stand. "Dad, I've never seen that ring. You can't make me say I did. You could pound the stuffing out of me, but I won't tell you that these guesses of yours are right, cause they're not." The challenge didn't really represent a danger. Dad had never touched him. Any spankings, back when he was little, had come from Mom.

The big fists closed, then opened. Dad's neck was flushed a deep red. "Jim, I believe that some-one with a February birthday is in that grave. I think you know it now, but you won't help me. It's only what I think, not what I can prove, and I'm not going out on that limb again after what happened in this house last summer. There's an old saying that you can't run with the hare and hunt with the hounds, and I guess you've made your choice. I'm not one to talk about how I love my family, but I do. My whole family. I love you, Jim, but you won't let me, and now you turn this way. I don't think there's truth between us, Jim, and the word love is just sentimental garbage without truth. Think about it."

Jim got up and walked out of the study. His face was burning, and he didn't want Dad to see. Somehow, his body was showing shame, while part of his mind was triumphant. Gramp had had an explosion in his brain after a confrontation no worse that this, but he had proved tougher. He had paid back for Gramp.

CHAPTER 10

Declarations of independence are sometimes as simple as that, the substitution of what you think is right for what someone else says is right. There was just no doubt in my mind that I was right in concealing what I knew about that ring, because I knew in my heart that Dad was wrong, that he was stubbornly holding on to an idea that had already caused so much trouble. The knowledge that Gloria Peet was in that grave was no longer an assumption. It had become an article of faith, a truth I shared with Gramp and the rest of the world against the delusion of my father. And the fact that he was vulnerable on this point made him vulnerable on every point to the logical mind of a fourteen year old.

It was probably fortunate that I didn't have much time to put my independence to the test of living together. Within three weeks I was off to Ipperwash cadet camp again, this time for over seven weeks, ten days of "standard" camp followed by six weeks of Driver-Mechanic training. I can still remember the strain of steering the old World War II sixty-hundredweight trucks, staring at the bottom of the windshield through the top arc of a wooden steering wheel — until my instructor insisted that I bring a pillow to raise my eighty pound body a few inches, a pillow I had to carry on morning parade, the lone pillow-carrier among twelve hundred cadets. My mother was a normal human being and my father was much larger than average; why was I cursed with slow growth? When I did finally "spurt" a year later, I was finally reconciled with my body, but I have never forgotten the feelings, and I have always understood something of the frustrations of small men and been wary of them.

When I returned to home, it had shifted from Kirkland Lake to Haileybury, and Dad was already away most of the time. Our name was well enough known in Haileybury that I found my position in the pecking order of Haileybury High School fairly easily. Socially, I was about five away from the bottom of Middle School (a room combining Grades Eleven and Twelve), and about five from the top academically. My search for mediocrity was finally paying off. I fell in love again, more platonically this time. I remember being proud of the purity of my emotions, happy that the burning of the previous year was, I thought, over.

I even achieved some financial independence, working in a downtown grocery store for seventy-five cents an hour, sixteen hours a week. Twelve dollars a week free and clear, no income tax UIC, CPP, air other deductions — and on the spending side, no GST, PST or other annoyances. I experimented with smoking, cautiously at first, since it was known to stunt growth. My love was not being requited, but that was almost welcome. She was going with a friend of mine, and the nobility of my self-sacrifice was consolation enough. Altogether, it was a very satisfying year.

Dad came home one weekend a month. I never flaunted my new independence, though I'm sure my jaunty "Heading downtown, see you later", after supper on Saturday must have sounded strange to him. Three hours of sitting in the Good Food Grill, ordering just enough at intervals to keep the owner at bay, was sophistication, even if I was clinging to the fringes of a faster crowd, Buster's, around the corner, had some space for dancing to the jukebox, and once in a great while I danced with the love of my life (she unaware of this status). When I arrived home, often after midnight, I would sometimes hear Dad's rumble of displeasure and Mom's soft placatory murmur. She kept the peace between us, I'm now sure, though at the time I thought it was my own forbearance.

Those weekends when Dad was home were generally weekends when Gramp would become more visibly ill, often holding to his bed for the whole two days. Sometimes, Dad had to carry him down to the car — to take him to the hospital for an X-ray or some procedure the doctor could not arrange at the house. I remember standing on the porch one winter day, watching them from behind. Dad's back was absolutely straight, no concession to the weight of his father in his arms. Gramp couldn't hold his back straight, but his one functioning arm would not go around the neck of his bearer, but rested on his lap, so that he sat like Charlie McCarthy, wooden and defiant. Dad wasn't rough or anything in settling Gramp in the car, but brusque, eager to get it over with. There was never a grunt of thanks from Gramp or an inquiry of "OK?" from Dad. Solicitude was left to Mom, Willy or me. She would extend it surreptitiously, Willy without any concern about how it looked, and me ostentatiously. Gramp would receive it with red face and eyes staring straight out the windshield. But come Monday, the house would return to an even tenor.

We checked Gramp into the hospital in June so that the four of us could go down to Toronto for Dad's graduation from Police College. He already knew that his first posting would be North Bay. Nana knew that the arrangements of the past year would have to change, and was thinking of moving to North Bay herself — I remember her and Mom talking about the possibility, both knowing that the combined household idea wouldn't be the same with Dad home, and Mom knowing that her own family had to come together.

So Gramp's death, coming in late September before any final decisions were made, came just in time. It was kidney failure, or at least the failure of some parts of him to come to terms, physically, with paralysis. I was fifteen by then, and sailed through the condolences at school and at the funeral in full Beau Geste style, stiff Gary Cooper upper lip and a conviction that, in the future, when all was known, people (particularly one girl) would know how well I had served my grandfather, no matter the cost to me.

Jim stared at the casket, the banks of flowers behind and around it, and the carved ivory face of the old man, his mouth finally straightened by the hands of the undertaker. Doctor after doctor had tried, and Gramp himself had attempted to focus the power of a strong will into lifting that right hand corner of his mouth. Only in death had the flesh yielded, relaxed, taken on the malleability of an actor.

There was a crucifix above the casket. Was Nana pretending that Gramp was a good Catholic? Surely God knew he wasn't, but it seemed a lot of good Catholics figured God could be fooled —"Yes, Lord, he would have been at mass every Sunday, but things kept cropping up. He really wanted to be there." Jim craned his neck to look at the people crowding into the funeral chapel. He couldn't put a name to most of them, these older people of Haileybury, some maybe from Cobalt, even Toronto. One thing he knew, and that was that very few people had visited Gramp in the past year and a half; that made a lot of people in this room hypocrites. Look at the crucifix! Tomorrow, it might be replaced by a simple cross, then the next day by a Star of David. Jim was starting to get very uncomfortable with religion and its ritual. Some nights, he and Kenny talked about what life was really all about, and there were a few times this past summer that Jim, staring at the stars hanging over the dinghy, had felt so lost in the immensity of the universe, so much a part of a totally mysterious plan that weekly things like Sunday mass just seemed to lose all their meaning.

The priest was talking. He was a thin, very dark and intense young French-Canadian from the pro-cathedral here in Haileybury. Father Laliberte, that was it. Mom, Jim and Willy had kept going to St. Patrick's in Cobalt while they were living with Nana and Gramp. This was mainly so that Mom could keep up with her CWL friends there, and it also gave Nana a quiet time at mass. Someone had to be in the house with Gramp anyway, so there was no way to go to mass all together. The priest was talking. What did they call it? Eulogy, that was it. To speak well. Dis-logy would be to speak ill of the dead. More hypocrisy. Jim heard only bits and pieces, sometimes distorted by French pronunciation, stilted and hesitant. "Mr. Thorpe was not a man I knew … well, but he was known far … more well by many of you here. He was a …" The next word sounded like ""pee on hyar" and it took Jim a couple of seconds to get it. "Pioneer".

"… of the industry of mining here in Temiskaming, an employer of many, and a man who gave generously to many causes." This surprised Jim, to whom Gramp had often expressed contempt for organized charity. He perked up his ears, but the priest did not get specific. Instead, he began to concentrate on Nana, who was obviously a mainstay of the parish here in Haileybury. Maybe that was the explanation, that Gramp had involuntarily supported causes, with Nana handling the money now. On he wandered verbally, only the mispronunciations causing slight currents of interest, quickly squelched, in the gathered mourners. Jim grew more indignant. It would be better to have some union firebrand up there, calling down anathema on Gramp for his suppression of the workers. He glanced sideways at his Dad, careful not to turn his head.

Dad's face was frozen, impassive. It looked like he was pressing the small of his back into the pew, for his whole upper body, that huge frame, seemed tense to the point of trembling. Jim could see his left eye, and he watched for a blink, getting to twenty-five before there was a twitch. Willy was between Jim and Dad, his thin dark face — why did he have to look like that priest? — intent on the face in the casket. Willy and Nana had cried, together and almost uncontrollably. Dad had just frozen. Mom? Had she loved Gramp? Jim didn't know, but he thought she respected the old man, returned the respect he had always shown her.

How about him? How did he really feel? Jim had felt allied with Gramp. He had felt waves of support from the wordless old man for his … defiance? Not really. It was resistance, a refusal to let Dad dictate his whole life, what he thought, who he spent time with. Now that Gramp was gone, would it make a difference in how Dad acted?

The funeral procession left the street outside the funeral home and rolled south. Jim was surprised when it rolled right past the turnoff to the Haileybury cemetery, and instead drove slowly towards North Cobalt. The leaves were turning now, mainly the poplars, great bands of yellow against the spruce, the odd maple punctuating the display with a splash of red. Lake Temiskaming slid away behind them, the bright mosaic of Burnt Island disappearing as the procession swung around the long curve, and the first houses of North Cobalt huddled up to the road. Jim turned to look at the procession, about twenty cars with their headlights on. The oncoming northbound traffic was pulling over to the shoulder and halting for the passage of the cortege. Through North Cobalt now. Finally the hearse made a left turn into the Cobalt cemetery.

"Why here?" he whispered to his mother as they walked from their car to stand beside the hearse. Dad was five steps ahead, as if eager to get it over with. Nana was following Dad, head down.

"I think we should be quiet on that right now. It's something your father said Gramp told him, but when I'm not sure. Nana's sort of in shock, and I don't know how this affects it. Don't say anything." All of this was in an urgent, low tone. Jim looked past the hearse, past the bustle at the back as the undertaker's two assistants got a folding cart ready. The sun was almost touching the trees on top of the slope to the west, over past the railway tracks. Some leaves, picked off a poplar by a little gust of wind, fluttered down on the hearse and the casket. Some cars had to park outside the gates, and people were filing in walking up the gentle slope beside the line of cars.

The grave was over to the left, with a pile of dirt to one side. The dirt was grey, and Jim, stretching, could see that the earth changed colour about a foot down. Clay. Half a mile either way and they would have found sandy loam. This was consecrated ground, but it was also the very devil to dig in. Ritual again. Why are we bound by it, he thought, when the body doesn't mean anything, really. Suddenly he felt a chill. The last time he'd been in this graveyard, he'd had that fantasy about Gloria Peet coming out of her grave to claim her ring. His view of the corner with her grave was blocked by a station wagon.

Near the open grave waiting for Gramp's body were some chairs and a sort of rug made out of fake bright green grass. The graves around looked tired, neglected, with long wisps of brown grass, leaves staring to pile against the headstones. Jim remembered that every spring — which in Cobalt meant early May — the priest in St.Pat's would announce that next weekend was cleanup day at the cemetery, everyone invited to come with rakes and clippers. That was probably when some busybody found that ring and caused all the trouble between him and Dad. Next year, they'd ask again for people to go out and tidy up, only then Gramp's grave would be one with growing grass and junk left from the melt, maybe sunk down in the spring, he'd heard that happened with graves.

The undertaker was making sweeping motions with his hand, indicating that the family had to lead the way over to the grave and wait for the casket to be brought. Mom took Nana's hand, and the two of them followed Dad, the two boys trailing. Impulsively, he took Willy's hand and gave it a squeeze. There was a sob beside him, but he didn't look down.

Dad positioned Nana in front of one of the chairs, then went around the row to stand behind her, his hand on her left shoulder. Mom stayed on her right. Willy broke free from Jim, and went to Mom's right. Jim paused at the end of the row of chairs and decided to stay where he was.

The coffin was lifted from the cart and slid onto some straps stretching over the grave. Jim saw that the straps were wound around steel rods, one on each side of the open hole, and that one of the under-taker's men was squatting by a lever. He remembered telling the Grade Eleven Latin class about Roman burial customs, the eyes being closed with coins, another coin put into the mouth to pay the boatman the fare to cross the river. What was the boatman's name? Charon, that was it. Cerberus was the dog with all the heads. This guy with the lever, he guessed, was Charon today. His real name was Donny Graham. He'd been in Grade Twelve in Cobalt High School three years ago. Maybe he figured that his only asset in life was an ability to look really mournful, and he'd started on this low rung of the profession.

Now the priest was saying something, reading it from a little black leather book. It went on and on, no words that Jim wanted to hear. Then the lever moved, Donny Graham made his grandfather's cof-fin jerk and subside, the straps moving unevenly for some reason, but always down. Jim jerked his gaze away, and looked out over the cemetery road.

There it was, Gloria Peet's grave. An island of neatness in a sea of neglect. Clipped, cleaned up, a little jar of flowers in front of the slate limestone.

Jim shook his head sharply and looked back at Gramp's coffin. Then he snuck a peek at everyone around, thinking that they all might have been watching him turn away from the ceremony. Everyone was watching the coffin make its jagged descent into the clay. Except Dad. His head was turned sharply to the right, and he was staring at Jim.

He felt his face burning like a maple in a bunch of poplars, knew that everyone must be watching the two of them. Nana wasn't, he saw. She bent down and picked up some earth — not, he noticed, a chunk of clay — and tossed it onto the casket in the grave. Mom put her arm around her, and Willy grabbed her hand and held it in his two small hands. Dad moved his gaze back to the grave. Nothing had happened, but Jim felt naked.

The shadows of the bush over to the west of the tracks were climbing across the road and sliding up into the cemetery as the first cars got turned around and back onto the highway. Everyone was stuck for a few minutes when an old couple — Haileybury? — almost hung their Lincoln up by backing into a ditch, but four men, including Donny, mourner and infernal boatman, heaved on the big bumper and gave the big car enough purchase to get moving again, Donny and the other Samaritans spattered with clay and loam. Nana was back with them now, Dad driving the Buick and Jim staring at the mus-cular neck in front of him, at the back of that big head, wondering.

There were about thirty people in the house for the next three hours.Casseroles were delivered to the back door in a stream, not continuous, but rhythmic. Jim was surprised. Haileybury was supposed to be quite without soul or sympathy. Certainly, no one came in, weeping and clutching Nana, but these offerings of beef, chicken and cheeses in baked dishes spoke of feeling. The fridge was packed, and the casseroles began to be marshalled on the porch. There would be frost tonight, that would be fine, Mom said.

Finally, about eight, the last ones left. Mom edged Nana up the stairs, and the boys could hear the quiet murmur of their voices for a long time. Jim longed to escape, and finally said "I'm going for a walk." His father just looked at him. Willy, sitting beside Dad on the sofa, looked so woebegone that Jim almost lost his resolve and offered to stay. He knew where he might find some friends tonight, and as he went from the pooled light of one streetlight into another, he rehearsed what he was going to tell them about the funeral, the emptiness of the ritual, the hypocrisy. But the image that stayed with him was of Willy and Dad sitting on the sofa, both staring at him.

CHAPTER 11

Much of our comfort level must rest on convenient forgetting. I've known for forty years that I "lost" my faith as a teenager, and I've traded on it: written stories about Catholicism and about priests with the confidence of a born insider combined with the "objectivity" of a self-made skeptic; swapped stories of parochial school torture with other survivors; slandered a whole vocation by making smug assumptions that celibacy equals perversion. Dee's death ripped my life apart, tearing away some of those layers of self-assurance, and now I'm cautiously, oh so cautiously, beginning to explore religion. I mean explore in the sense of entering unknown country, not whipping through it on some limited access highway labelled "Ecumenicism" or "Spirituality".

Willy, this whole thing is addressed to you if anyone, though I'm still not sure if you will ever see it. You were there at the funeral, just turned ten, and I was there, almost sixteen, and what a difference there was! You drew closer, to Dad, to Nana, to Mom, and I pulled away. All that crap of feeling part of some inexpressible immensity and therefore above the rituals that keep us humans aware of our place in the … I was about to use a catch phrase, "the scheme of things", but I'll substitute … process of becoming real. You stayed on track, I didn't, and maybe it was ritual that helped you. I became so much more concerned with how I looked to other people that I put everything into creating my own surface. Actually, many surfaces, "The Man of a Thousand Skins", the professional me, the convivial me, the confidante me, so many mes that I stretched very thin. Dee found a little bit of my centre and took care of it so it wouldn't die, but for the rest of the world I had to keep that great extended surface in good repair.

To be honest … how often does that phrase open a patently dishonest statement? I want to be honest, but I'm not sure I have the capacity. That's quite a confession for someone who became rather well known for hard-hitting journalism. But that was just one of my skins, albeit one of the thickest. Anyway, if I am to be honest, if I must tell the truth to you, Willy, through this document, then I have to say that my "exploration" of religion is highly tentative right now. I've actually been to mass a few times in the last year.

The first time was with Marjorie. She's a very nice lady whom I met on a foray Roger insisted on dragging me on, a visit to a tea dance at a seniors' centre a few miles down island. Within minutes, I realized I was highly marketable. Vancouver Island must be one of the most widow-intensive regions of Canada, and I seemed to arouse reactions ranging from predatory to motherly. Marjorie stood out because she seemed interested in me as an adult, not as potential material. We talked and danced, and I felt some honest (that word again!) enjoyment in company, the first for a long time. She asked me where I went to church — asked it without offence and in such a way that I could have turned her away without offence — and I found myself explaining that I was once Catholic. She said "Once is always" with such assurance that I had to laugh. Anyway, it led to an invitation to go to her church with her on Sunday, two days away.

I found a strange world there. Of course, I did not expect to be drawn back to the Latin mass of my youth Ad Deum qui laetificat juventutem meum, to God who gives joy to my youth. I knew, had even reported on, many of the changes in the church, the use of the vernacular, the growth in lay participation, all of those things. What I was unprepared for was the relaxed atmosphere, the blurring of lines which had once been boundaries between sacred and profane. People spoke, out loud, on the way down the aisle, about the weather, their visitors, their ailments. There were a few quips in the sermon (now called a homily, a word which somehow brings an image of cereal), and actual laughter in the congregation (and here I almost used the word audience). Coffee and cookies in the bright adjacent parish hall, a sister ("nun" seems to be an outmoded word) who would fit in at a feminist meeting: it was all a little disorienting. Yet Marjorie and the others were obviously believers in an omnipotent, omniscient God, they took God into their mouths using their own hands to bear Him there, all as if it were the most normal thing in the world.

Since then, I've done a little shopping. I found a Portuguese church down in Victoria where the mass in the vernacular sounded a little more like Latin, where the older congregation, mostly little old ladies in black, looked more like the people in St. Patrick's in Cobalt. I took communion, worried a little about retribution for the years of neglect. I talked with a retired priest in Qualicum Beach, but so guardedly that he told me to go away and decide a few things on my own before getting to the nitty gritty, as he called it.

So there is my spiritual state at the moment, terra incognita. The frightening thing is that I got this way through simple self-neglect masquerading as tough minded skepticism. So I've got to be careful, just like in this narrative. I've noticed in the past few weeks that I'm dragging things out in several senses: dragging the memories, more reluctantly, out in fragments separated by days and days of nothing. September now.

Anyway, the sight of the grave — not Gramp's but Gloria Peet's — shook me that day. Somebody cared about the set of remains I had found down in the mine. Maybe there was a childhood friend of hers in Cobalt, someone who had kept her mouth shut during the summer her body was discovered, kept quiet then but returned every so often to tend the grave. Maybe that was the person who found the ring last spring. For a minute there beside Gramp's grave, even while the casket was dropping, Gloria Peet became a person for me because someone else cared about her.

It was after I had that memory about Gramp's funeral that I had a dream about Dee. She and I were here, in Parksville, in this house. It was during her illness, I could tell that, but she wasn't in any pain; in fact, there wasn't even apprehension. We seemed to be planning something together, and she sent me out to get something. "You'll know it when you see it." she said, and gave me that incredibly sweet grave smile she never lost. Anyway, off I went, to find that a huge new shopping centre had appeared, seemingly overnight, right on the beach about a mile north of our intersection with the Island Highway. I started with a big hardware store, and was drawn into the seasonal goods section, then gardening. It had something to do with seeds, so I stood looking at a rack of seed packets for a while. Then I saw a sign for real estate on top of the next rack. There was a pile of little packaged cubes, about three inches to a side, each showing a picture of a house or a cottage.. I picked one up at random, a side-split suburban house with a sweeping lawn in the picture, looking about twenty-five hundred square feet, four bedrooms with rec room — that sort of thing. The side of the box had planting instructions. There wasn't really too much to choose from in the rack, so I took the side-split and paid for it with my Visa. I was home in a dream-flash with my purchase, showing it to Dee like a kindergarten kid with some refrigerator art. Then we had a fight.

Or I had a snit. Dee just pointed out some information on the side about growing zones in Canada, and how this particular house just wouldn't work. I insisted it would and pulled the box from her hands. There was a shovel in the shed, and I was going to get this thing planted NOW.

Outside, it was about zero. The sun was a faint nimbus over the mountains to the west, and there was a dirty sleet coming in on a northwest wind. But I was angry, and when I'm angry, I'm pretty stubborn. I grabbed the spade and chose a spot in the back yard that normally gets a lot of sun. I'd show her: I drove the spade into the ground, about two inches, and hit something hard. Must be a stone. I tried again a few inches away. Another jarring stop. I wound up clearing about four square feet of sod away to reveal chalky hardpan. There was no way I could get down the two feet the planting instructions called for. I admitted defeat and went in to consult with Dee. As I entered the house, the wind dropped, the sun came out and streamed in from the patio, and a rainbow formed.

Back to the hardware store, though the shopping centre seemed to have moved a bit farther north. "Something more appropriate," Dee had murmured. It took some hunting, but I found an A-frame cottage in a box.

Of course, that didn't work either. I should have known this thing was going to work in threes, two unsuccessful tries before things happened right. This time I hit roots, hundreds of intertwined woody roots inches below the surface of the back yard. Dee was sympathetic, but tiring. I had to do this thing right.

The third box was a playhouse, like a treehouse. The doors and windows were about three-quarter scale, but there was only one room. This time, Dee approved fully, and there was no trouble in the planting. I went to sleep in my dream, and woke in the real world. I felt like Jack, and almost rushed out to see my beanstalk house.

I thought about that dream most of the day, trying to draw it up beside my memories and find points of comparison. Finally, I realized that dreams are more likely about memories to come than about the ones you've already reviewed. In this string of memories from my youth, I've been becoming more familiar with Jimmy/Jim/Me, more identified. Now I seem to be more in control, at least of the start point of a memory. For example, I remember, in the conventional sense, a family discussion two days after Gramp's funeral, one that had to do with houses.

Dad was starting with the OPP detachment in North Bay, living in the basement of another constable. He had to go back on Tuesday, and that was the subject of a family conference on Sunday, on our way back from mass in Cobalt. It took place in a red leatherette booth in the Good Food Grill. Nana wasn't supposed to hear, and so we crowded in there, the only time our entire family ever sat together in a restaurant.

Jim fiddled with the salt and pepper shakers, drawing circles on the damp table surface. Dad ordered pop for Willy and Jim, coffee for himself and Mom, and we all waited in silence while the waitress got the whole thing straight and brought the order. Then Mom started.

"Dad's got to go back to the Bay on Tuesday, early. I'll be going with him. You boys can look after Nana, right?" Willy's eyes were big, and his nod was slow and exaggerated Jim just shrugged. She continued, "I'll be looking for an apartment for the first year."

There was one apartment house in Haileybury, and several in Kirkland Lake, and it was from these that the boys drew their pictures of what "an apartment" meant. In Cobalt, there were only three categories of dwellings: rooming houses, shacks, and regular houses. An apartment meant no yard, no basement, no attic. Only later did Jim realize it also meant no woodpile, no furnace, no lawn to mow. But he understood why they were deciding on one. Dad's first posting would probably only last a year to a year and a half.

Mom was going on. "Jim, how do you feel about switching schools? He had been worrying about that, with Grade Thirteen started only a month before. He was finally a respectable height for a teenager, having moved from squirt to beanpole in a matter of months. A pair of pants, drapes, carefully selected for their forty inch knees and fifteen inch cuffs, would look sharp for about a week, and then his socks would start to show. But he was playing football for the first time, on the junior team as a fifteen year old, and even then the lightest boy on the team at ninety-three pounds. The coach, philosophical about forging senior and junior football teams out of a total pool of sixty-four boys in the school, had not automatically rejected him, but had placed him as an end. Unfortunately, the growth spurt had brought with it no speed, no grace, and no sureness of hand. Some of their least used plays involved forward passes to the end. But he was on the field — everybody was, all the time — and Jim knew that in North Bay he would be a spectator. Basketball would start in month, and he might make the junior team in that. Same coach, of course, the only male teacher in the school, besides the principal.

"I'd rather finish Grade Thirteen here."

"I thought so. And that might help us with a problem."

Jim shot a glance at Dad's face. Dad was staring at the sugar container as if trying to penetrate its mysteries. For a moment, looking at that worried face, that big frame scrunched into the far corner of the booth, he felt sorrow. Then he remembered that it was Dad who started this fight or whatever it was, and he looked back at Mom beside him. "Problem?" A challenge. What do you mean, I'm a problem? The real problem is that nobody leaves me alone to think my own thoughts. He looked at Willy. Poor kid doesn't know how hard parents can be on you.

"Yes, Nana. We don't think she should be left alone right now. But Dad can't keep living in that basement room, coming up here the odd weekend. We've got to find a compromise."

"You mean a *modus vivendi*." Way of living — for someone who'd almost dropped Latin last year, Jim was quick with a tag. Mom smiled.

"Sort of. We thought if you could stay here the rest of the school year, and provide her with ... companionship, someone to talk to, and help around the house. She and Gramp were married over forty years."

Jim felt almost light-headed with the relief going through his body, almost a physical tingle. Perfect! He'd get to stay here, Dad would be there with all that disapproval, he could play basketball, stay where he could see HER every day (though never speak his love, like *Beau Geste*) and live in a real house, not an apartment. He forced his face to stay still, and moved the salt shaker a complete circle around the pepper.

"You would be the man of the house." When Mom said this, Dad's head jerked back and he stared at Jim. Was that contempt? Jim was tempted to flare, but he just tightened his grip on the two shakers and felt his face burning. He had to get that under control.

"Mom," he started. He was damned if he was going to address Dad right now. "You're right." Long pause. "It would be good from my point of view. I mean, Grade Thirteen is going now, and to switch schools… they sometimes don't cover stuff in the same order." No point talking about football or basketball, Dad would probably laugh. Academics counted, though, with someone who hadn't finished high school. He wasn't trying to fool Mom particularly, just keeping the emphasis right. "And Nana, you know, I'd take good care, like I'd want to, she's so … upset now."

Willy was looking at him, and, he realized, was seeing right through the act, the whole thing. Willy's face was starting to crumple, as if some object were flying right towards his eyes. Couldn't help that now. The next few minutes would decide his fate for the year: freedom or cooped up in some dinky little apartment in North Bay, going to that big collegiate, where probably the junior teams were picking guys three times his size. Willy would be OK.

So far. Dad hadn't said a thing. Now he slid the sugar container over to the wall by the menus, but it went so fast that it bounced off and turned over, some sugar coming out and spreading across the table in a little spray, fan-shaped. "Well. that's decided. Let's go." Mom looked at him, and her lips tightened. Jim realized that this had been Mom's idea, that she did the talking because she had told Dad it was the only way it would work. She looked back at Jim and smiled, but it wasn't her real smile, it was a compact smile, a contract smile that said I've saved your bacon young fella, don't mess it up now. Willy was actually crying, though nobody but Jim could see. Mom was concentrating that smile on Jim, Dad was shifting so that Willy slid along the seat, and only Jim could see those two tears going down his thin cheeks. Then Willy wiped them away with his sleeve, and everybody kept moving, out of the booth, out of the Good Food Grill, out into the crystalline fall sun shining on Ferguson Street in Haileybury that bright October Sunday.

CHAPTER 12

Ordinarily I doze on a plane. After all, it used to be my way of getting to my job, and somebody else is driving. But this is one of those early fall days when the country below just shines. We're over the prairies now, and I'm not getting as much into the laptop as I could; my eyes keep drifting to the earth below.

As I look back over this journal, I realize that what started months ago as an exercise in memory — well, really an attempt to restrain a rampant memory — has impinged more and more on my waking life. I thought of writing the experience down as a way of controlling it. In the past, I have confined civil wars, atrocities, famines, mass suicides to the neat margins of the printed page. My justified print, my justified life. If a piece was falling a hundred words short, just turn up the indignation, undelete a few adjectives and adverbs. A little long? Restrain it, take out a few of the clauses that hint at greater complexity, boil down to the central theme, but make sure the theme is unique to J. Thorpe, columnist and journalist, pundit. Keep the angle sharp and unexpected.

So young Jimmy has been my subject. Notice how careful I have been to keep the distance? That's objectivity for you. No one can claim that I, the journalist, feel personally involved. Except I am, except I am, except I am. Hamlet is only happy at one point in that play, and that's when he's got the players to be his intermediaries, when he's able to withdraw to the relatively safe position of the director/stage manager. Now I think I have to go to the scene of the action. Particularly, I have to talk with Willy. He knows I'm coming, but not why.

When Dad died in 1985, I was in South America, working on a series of articles on revolutionary movements, trying to find the common threads tying Sandinistas to Shining Path. There weren't many, common threads that is, but that was my thesis, and columnists are supposed to go behind the facts. Sometimes way behind. By the time I got to North Bay, Dad had already been cremated. If I felt any grief, it was for myself. Dad had been gone a long time. the dementia of Alzheimers had removed the man from the shell almost two years before. His last words had been in late 1983, and the last ones to make much sense months before that.

He got good care in Cassellhome, in the Special Care Unit there. Willy made a point of getting down from Timmins at least once a month, and I got there with about half that frequency. At that time, Dee and I were based in Mississauga, though both of us were travelling a lot. If we saw a few days free, we'd head north.

I remember one visit, in the fall of 1984, ten years ago, practically to the day. dad was slumped in his chair, held from sliding out by some straps. His eyes were closed. Everything was slack, deflated, like a collapsed tent. The nursing aide who wheeled him in was young, about twenty-three or twenty-four, quite pretty. She checked the brakes on his chair, then put her hands under his armpits to hoist him up a bit, quickly adjusting a pillow. A towel under one strap had slipped, and she loosened the strap slightly to replace the towel, then snugged it tight. "Your son is here to visit, Mr. Thorpe. It's a beautiful day." She turned to Dee and me. "You might want to wheel him outside. Just use those sliding doors. If you do, I'd suggest not more than twenty minutes out there." She looked back at

Dad. Sunlight was hitting his face, though his eyes didn't open or his eyelids move. The aide went over and adjusted some venetian blinds.

"How has he been?"

She came closer, and her voice dropped to a confidential murmur. "No real change, outwardly." She turned and looked at him. "Such a shame. He was a big man, wasn't he? I saw his picture in his room, one in uniform. It's a terrible disease, but I don't think he's aware of any discomfort. We always hope."

I lowered my own voice, ashamed. This young girl was more careful of my father's dignity than I was. "How is he eating?"

"Pretty well. His swallowing reflexes are still OK. It's mainly a matter of getting the spoon in, and rhythm. Once he's started, he does quite well. Circulation is always a problem. We shift him back and forth, bed, chair, and then of course there's his bath and the physio. WE don't want sores to get a start. I remember when he first came — it was my first month here too. A real gentleman. He never let the confusion get in the way of being polite and considerate." She smiled brightly at Dad. "Have a good visit with your son, Mr. Thorpe. I'll be back in an hour."

Later, driving down Highway 11, I said to Dee, "It must get awfully tiring, being cheerful like that nurse, in a place like that."

"Maybe it's vital. If you were working there and started thinking of it as a place for used up humans, it would be really depressing. You could see she wasn't just treating him with dignity; she really believed in his dignity, always acting as if he could see, hear and understand. I guess an act would wear out, so they just have to make sure that they get true believers. Lord, if it ever happens to me, I hope I get a place like that."

Dee was in China when he died, and with me in South America, Ken, at seventeen had to represent our family. Willy handled all the arrangements, but by the time I got to North Bay, he had to be getting back to his school in Timmins. We had only about an hour together.

"Strange," I said to Willy, "but when I try to visualize Dad, it's like one of those holographic images, you know, where there's two pictures, one replacing the other as you shift your point of view so much as an inch. One image of him lying in that bed in the Special Care Unit, nothing much to him, no reaction for almost two years, and then the other image of him as town policeman in Cobalt, so huge and powerful."

"You really had a hard time getting along with him, didn't you, Jim? I mean, i DON'T mean that you hated him or anything like that, just that your two surfaces were … sort of like those little magnetic dogs, you know, the Scotties, one black, one white, and when you moved on, the other one would zip away. You and Dad just had different polarities. But you loved him and he loved you. He used to talk about you, after he retired, and he kept a scrapbook of all the things you wrote for the Globe and Macleans. He talked about how smart you were in school. But he never said why you fought. That was around the time that Mom died, wasn't it?"

"Before that. That thing at Mom's funeral … it wasn't really him, wasn't really me. It had to do with Gramp, mainly. But it's dead now. They're all dead now. What's that Bible quote, 'Let the dead bury the dead'? Let's drop it, OK, Willy?"

A man of tact, Willy did. But he did leave me with a small task. "Over at Cassellhome, they're holding a suitcase full of papers — including that scrapbook. Can you go through it? I've already passed his clothes on to Goodwill Industries, and I took his medals over to the Algonquin headquarters here in North Bay. But maybe the papers can be yours to sort out." And then we went outside, and I waved to him as he took off in his Honda Civic. I felt ashamed, yes, to have turned him off so abruptly. Maybe I should have confessed that I'd treated Dad … shabbily? No, distantly, cautiously. Even the last time I'd seen him, a wraith in a hospital bed, I'd had the feeling that he might rise up and smite me.

I picked up the suitcase. Some of the staff came over and told me how sorry they were. The young girl Dee and I had met wasn't there; I asked, and was told she had moved to Toronto with her husband. "Andrea is a natural in this work. She's working at a home in Scarborough, and I hope she's appreciated." I said I hoped so too, seized the suitcase, and left.

The townhouse in Mississauga was empty of course. Dee was somewhere on the Yangtze, Ken was back at Upper Canada, and Laura had not come east from Edmonton, not that she should have. I ran around, turning on every light in the place, chasing the gloom. The suitcase sat in the hall, and, after a drink, I brought it into the living room. No lock, no precautions, it just opened like a … sandwich? small child? Dammit, it opened like a suitcase, it was just a suitcase.

The papers were a record of a quarter century of policing, of trying to get fellow citizens to do what they had agreed to do, covenanted by virtue of living here. Lots of carbons of arrest reports: Dad was canny enough to know that anything can come back to haunt you, and documentation should be ready. They were in those long transmittal envelopes, the ones with little strings that tie to red cardboard buttons, and each envelope had a year marked on it. They started in 1952 — I guess it was a technique he picked up at Police College. I peeked in a couple. The 1957 one had a Hilroy notebook init, an abbreviated diary, about five days to the page, when he went on duty, mileage, major events.

One envelope was almost empty, and it didn't have a year on it. Big block letters proclaimed "PETER THORPE SR. d 1951." There were lots of notations in the little columns on the front, organized by years. 1933, for example, had six little ditto marks below it, and numbers 1 to 7 to the right. Not every year had entries; they began in 1933, skipped 1934 and 1935. Then there was a big gap, 1941 to 1946, the war years I guessed. The envelope was worn and stretched. At one point it had been fat, but now there was only one item in it. I shook it out.

It was the last will and testament of Peter Thorpe, dated in early 1950, about eighteen months before his death. I balanced the will in my hand, and decided that reading it would not betray anyone or anything. I knew its broad outlines anyway.

Gramp had settled a life annuity on Nana, Catherine Bowden Thorpe, and the house and personal effects, noting that she could expect a substantial income from the annuity. The executors of the estate were my father and his sister, Evelyn Thorpe. Until Evelyn was found, my father was to act as sole executor, with the advice of so-and-so from the Bank of Nova Scotia. And he was enjoined to seek diligently for the whereabouts of his sister Evelyn Thorpe, so that she could take up her duties.

Willy and I were mentioned, each getting a bequest of $30,000 to further our studies. I'd known about that and claimed it when I started university. Willy had, too.

The later part of the will spelled out what was meant by "diligently". The income from the residual estate was to be earmarked for the search for Evelyn. I knew Gramp, certainly knew how tightly he could clutch a coin before passing it along. Here he was, devoting his estate to the recovery of a lost daughter. Dad was to search for her for a period of not less than five years, but I knew he had kept it up longer. I also knew that after Mom's death, the residual estate had disappeared — not been spent, just disappeared, probably given to charities. It was as if Dad were washing himself clean of some contamination. Now, twenty-five years later, looking at the will, I felt resentment. On Willy's behalf, I told myself, Dee and I didn't need the money, but Willy could have used it, or Ken and Laura. Dad and Gramp were two stubborn men. There was Gramp, showing his belief that Evelyn could be found. There was Dad, doing … what?

I closed the suitcase and moved it to the basement. A few years later, when Dee and I were moving to the Island, I shipped it up to Willy, saying maybe it shouldn't be destroyed. He did have a big basement and wouldn't mind. When Nana died, back in 1972, he'd taken that stuff she'd left in storage in Haileybury.

The plane was banking now, far out over Lake Ontario. We'd lost three hours in time zones, and the lights of Toronto were coming on. I was going to rent a car at Pearson, but spend the night with Gwen and Charlie. They still live in Mississauga, in a condo high-rise now. Good friends then, good friends now, though the absence of Dee is palpable whenever we get together. I could see our old neighbourhood over to the left, south of 401, though I couldn't quite make out our street, the row of townhouses or the one second from the western end where I sat that night nine years ago and read that will. God, it seems the resentment will never die.

The visit with Gwen and Charlie was good, and I got on the road early. I have no clear idea what I'm going to say to Willy, but I'm starting to realize that spontaneity is going to be crucial in getting me out of this spin. I'll just take it slow, take time to think on the way. It's a familiar road. I remember the year after I graduated from high school, when I was working at Connaught Labs here in Toronto. I used to hitch-hike north at least every other weekend. My graduation was not filled with academic glory. "Taking care of Nana" had actually left me a lot of social freedom, so much that my marks slid to mediocrity. I dropped the one math I was taking and took up Latin again instead. The result was a hodge podge of courses that would barely have gotten me into university if I had wanted to go, which I didn't. I was sick and tired of being the youngest and smallest of every group.

Nana was a lot more independent than anyone gave her credit for, so when I packed up and headed for fame and fortune in Toronto, she didn't mind. Dad was posted to the Huntsville detachment that year. You could tell he thought I'd be back with my tail between my legs pretty quickly: the man who ran away from home at fifteen couldn't believe that a seventeen (almost) year old boy could survive out there. That increased my determination. So Marcel and I had gone to Toronto, survived in some pretty sad rooming houses, brushed up against poverty, including a week of real hunger, but survived.

My little green rental Neon cruised up Highway 400. It had just opened when I was in Toronto in 1953, and it was a hitch-hiker's nightmare. For the first time in history, a northbound driver leaving Toronto could get up some speed and maintain it. I learned to take the Yonge streetcar up to the end of the line and hitch up Highway 11. You'd get a lot of short rides, ten, fifteen miles, but it was better than watching the cars zipping by on 400.

Soon I was north of Barrie, and as I crested a hill, I saw the big red brick church on the west side of the highway. I had stood opposite that church for two hours one night in the summer of 1953, in a light rain, my thumb stuck out uselessly. I even remember what a fine state of indignation I was in.

The truck that stopped was so heavily loaded that it had barely made it up the hill, chugging at just over a walking pace. Truckers were good for rides, particularly late at night, for they wanted the company, the conversation, to stay awake. This driver was about fifty, with three or four days of grey beard showing. He was a chainsmoker, and practically his first act was to offer Jim a smoke. Jim's were wet, everything was wet, probably even the stuff in his bag was wet.

"Where ya headin' kid?"

"Huntsville."

"Be there by one or so. I'll be bunking down in South River, at Happy Landing. You know it?" Jim did. Every truck on Highway 11 stopped there, it seemed. He shivered in his wet clothes. It would be good to get into a warm house. Maybe he'd put off the confrontation with Dad till morning.

ON Wednesday, at coffee break, he'd seen the ad in Rosie's newspaper. He and Larry had just finished the first insulin test of the day, 192 mice injected with insulin and put in the warm boxes until an hour passed or they convulsed, whichever came first. Three boxes, or thirty six mice for the plant quality control, and all the rest were experiments, tests of experimental solutions, some from natural insulin, some artificial stuff. Inject, into the box, at least twelve mice a minute, start a new box each minute so your timing records stayed straight. By the time you got the thirteenth box finished, they were convulsing in the first boxes, and then it was pick 'em out, inject with sugar, save the poor little guys from coma and death. Finally, at the end, some sugar for all the ones that hadn't convulsed. Each test was an hour and a half of fast, picky work. Two more tests today, then three of Thursday, three on Friday and then the weekend. Sure, there were other things to do, the dogs downstairs for cortisone, the rabbits, the monkeys, the guinea pigs. But the mice and the insulin tests were how you measured the week.

The ad was in the personals, but it stood out as a boxed ad. What caught his eye was the phone number. His. Well, Dad's, Mom's, Willy's to be exact because he didn't live in Huntsville, didn't even have a phone here in Toronto. There it was, big and eye-catching:

REWARD FOR INFORMATION
LEADING TO LOCATION OF
EVELYN MARIE THORPE
BORN COBALT ONTARIO
FEBRUARY 15, 1917
MISSING SINCY JULY 1933
PHONE COLLECT
HUNTSVILLE 4691

What was Dad doing? Jim shook his head and read the thing again. He could have sworn that Dad thought Evvy was dead. Could it be Mom doing this? No, she would never work behind Dad's back.

The more he thought about it, the more confused and angry he got. This was 1953, twenty years. Why couldn't things just be dropped? If Dad thought she was alive, and why waste money on this ad if he didn't, then what the hell was all that business with the ring about? And if he did think she was alive, why the fight with Gramp? This must mean the two had agreed she wasn't dead. Jim knew Gramp had mentioned her in the will, but Nana never made it clear, and you couldn't push her on that topic — she'd just get all sad and weepy. He couldn't ask Dad, and didn't want to ask Mom.

Anyway, it was crazy. By Friday, Jim was sure that he had been meant to see that ad, that Dad was rubbing something in. He'd brought his bag, mostly laundry as usual, to work so he could get on the road quickly. He grabbed a doctor's sample pack of Dexedrine from the staff room. Had to stay awake on the road cause truckers didn't pick you up to watch you sleep. He'd get up to Huntsville and have it out once and for all.

The truck dropped him at the light in Huntsville, three blocks from the small house Mom and Dad had rented for the year. There was that huge house up in Haileybury with Nana all by herself, and here was her huge son and his family crammed into a two bedroom cottage. It was after midnight. Maybe downgrades had pushed the old truck along, for they were half an hour ahead of schedule. There was a light on in the bedroom. No car. Dad must be on shift.

He let himself in and called, "Mom? She was used to this on a Friday night, though if it was really late, he'd curl up on the sofa.

She came out in her dressing gown. "Look at you. Did you swim up from Toronto? Better get changed. There's some of your old clothes in the bottom drawer of the bureau in Willy's room. Don't wake him."

He shivered as he got into the dry pants and the old sweater. Mom had some coffee going when he came out. "Dad on shift?"

"Yes, he's working a double. Tourist season, and two guys are on course."

"Well, I guess I'll have to talk with him in the morning, if he's not too tired."

She sat and looked at him. "Jim, you're funny. Most weekends you come up and act like your father doesn't exist, like he doesn't earn the food you shovel down. Now, you're going to have a TALK, real important man stuff, I'll bet. What's going on?"

His wet jacket was hanging behind the kitchen door, and he got the ad from his pocket. It was wet, too, almost disintegrating. He put it in front of her on the table, and she looked at it. "Oh, that."

His anger boiled up. "Yes, that. I'd like to know what's going on." He was leaning on the table, both hands fisted, knuckles down on the wood. "Dad's doing this crazy thing …"

He never saw it coming, never dreamed his mother could move that fast or with such strength. She slapped him, full hand on the side of his face. He spun away, his foot slipped, and down he went to the kitchen floor. His face was numb, then a burning sting started.

"Don't you ever, ever, say that sort of thing about your father. And don't show your smug little face around here until you're prepared to think a little. I don't pretend to know every thing that goes on — not like you — but I do know he's the sanest, kindest man in our world. Now make up your mind, Jim. If you stay here, it's as a son, not some … investigator." She spat the last word out.

He got up. He might have known she'd be on that side of the fence. Even though Dad probably hadn't told her what he was thinking either. He turned and grabbed his jacket, then headed for the door, expecting her to call him back. He was almost at the street when the door opened again behind him.

"Jim?" He stopped and turned. "No, I'm not calling you back. It's best you not be here this weekend. Come back in a week or two. But on condition. You are not to bring this topic up. Understand?" He did. She was on Dad's side. He knew that hitch-hikers stranded in Huntsville, or in any of the towns along this route, could usually bunk in the police station, if there were cells free. Huntsville still had a town force, not OPP, and he'd probably get a bed, a bit firm, but a bed. However, he was Corporal Thorpe's son, so that option was out. He wandered to the outskirts of town and found a shed in a small farm lot. There were a couple of tarpaulins folded on the floor. It would do.

In the morning, he hitched up to Haileybury. Nana was surprised to see him, but pleased, he thought. At least someone was willing to take him as he was. He slept the whole afternoon, then went out with some of the guys in the evening. Nana insisted on giving him bus money to get back to Toronto.

On Wednesday, he got a letter from Mom

.

> Dear Jim,
>
> I am sorry for some things, mainly hitting you like that. It is possible you didn't mean what I thought I'd heard, and even if you did, striking someone in the face is an awful thing. I'm also sorry that I don't have the capacity to clear things up between you and Dad — not the knowledge, maybe not the skill.
>
> But I'm not sorry for making you leave. You cannot be in this house and set your face against the householder. When you come, you must come with respect for your father.
>
> We both love you. I can say it more easily than he can. Sometimes you make it a little difficult even for me.
>
> Mom

He pondered not answering for a week, but broke down.

> Dear Mom.
>
> I'm sorry too. I didn't know what I was talking about, I guess. I still don't.
>
> Don't worry about the slap. I'll get worse than that before I'm thirty!
>
> Maybe it would be best if I don't come up for a few weeks, and all of us an calm down.
>
> I love you too, and Dad.
>
> Jim

That sounded dignified and apologetic enough.

CHAPTER 13

I read a novel last month, a Canadian novel. One character was described as being "a voyeur of his own life". I'm starting to feel a little like him, but for different reasons. He had a "parched" existence, and I won't admit to that. But I am getting a definite sense of watching my life through a peephole.

The worst of it is that I am identifying with seventeen year old Jim Thorpe, even though I'm starting to dislike him. But his feelings are my feelings, his hurt pride just like mine. I can still see the dawn from that shed in Huntsville, still feel the shock of my mother's slap. And, with all that feeling, I'm still damned if I can remember exactly why Jim was so indignant about that advertisement. Gloria Peet may be on my mind now, but she certainly wasn't on Jim's. What he did know was that Evvy's whereabouts and circumstances were at the root of Dad and Gramp's enmity, and that he had taken Gramp's side. The only thing he had to feel guilty about was his defiance of his father, and he refused to feel or act guilty. Therefore Dad must be the guilty one. Projection, the psychologists call it.

Projection. That reminds me of a time I was giving a lecture to some journalism students at Western, sort of a guest shot. I'd brought along a 16mm film, a mixture of news clips I'd narrated and some outtakes. The idea was to explain criteria for inclusion. The students had some sheets noting the shot sequences, so I wouldn't have to be shutting down the projector and turning up the lights twenty-eight times during the fifteen minute film. I was watching the screen of course and keeping up a running commentary, and I was completely unaware that the take-up reel wasn't working. The film was running through and piling up behind me in a tangled heap.

That's the feeling I'm getting about my memory playbacks now. The first few, the summer of 1949, were very real, but, as I've said before, distanced , and not under my control. These more recent ones are where I should feel some control, and I do in terms of calling them up, but where they go, the consequences, are piling up in some sort of tangle, and I'm starting to feel a little desperate about it.

Driving always calms me. I had pulled off the road to stare at that old church in Oro, and I kept heading north. I pulled into Huntsville and tried to identify where that little house was. I'm pretty sure it is where some Toronto exurbanite has his tennis courts now, I recognized a tree that I'd leaned against staring back at the house forty-one years ago.

North of Huntsville, the four lane highway ends, and from there to the North Bay bypass, there's less change in the look of the road. I know it well, for I've hitch-hiked along it perhaps a hundred times, counting my years at university, my summers in Camp Borden, and the time I've just been remembering, those two years between high school and university. Here's Sunridge, where the girl of my dreams (and only of my dreams) spent her summers while in high school. There's the curve about halfway between Sunridge and South River. They've built a huge high school there, out in the bush, maybe two houses in sight. South River, the big gas station called Happy Landing where all the truckers would stop, and you could usually negotiate a ride. Trout Creek, where I walked one snowy night past a mile of lumberyard. Hitch-hiking was chancy in those days, but only in the sense of being unscheduled. Eight times out of ten, a bus would be faster, but there were those two times when you could feel you'd won a race. Now it's chancy in another sense. I don't pick up hitch-hikers now. Something, the drugs perhaps, or maybe a general psychosis of the times, has multiplied the sociopaths in our world. Once, six or seven years ago, I broke my own rule and picked up two guys who looked like they might freeze out there. The whole next hundred kilometres, I had this prickly feeling at the back of my neck. I couldn't see the one in the back seat. Was he preparing a knife? A garotte? It turned out, of course, that he was sleeping. But, given what we see on the news, my feeling was not unjustified.

The new bypass takes you well wide of Callander, the Quints' town. Well, actually they were born out in Corbeil, but the doctor came out from Callander, and that's where the highway and the railway were, so it got the credit. The first great rumblings of the Publicity Machine, or the first to affect us, Canadians out of the Toronto orbit. I wonder what the reporters of the Thirties would have made of Gloria Peet's body in the mine, or the reporters of today's tabloids. I can see the headlines: "Sleeping Beauty", "Ice Maiden". Is it just that the mores of one's own youth seem more sensible? Maybe the reporters of the late forties and early fifties had been shocked into restraint by the horrors of World War II. But since then, we've had the drip, drip, drip of horror, the Congo, Biafra, Vietnam, Bangladesh, Cambodia, Ethiopia, Sudan, Somalia, Angola, Mozambique, Afghanistan, Argentina, Nicaragua, Jonesville, Waco, Bosnia, Haiti, and no sign of it stopping. Maybe now we're so desensitized that the tabloids are justified in their screaming, like relatives of a man slowly going deaf, whose voices creep up in volume over the years.

In North Bay, the bypass skirts the eastern edge of town. Cassellhome is visible from the highway, and my eyes swung to it, for it was my father's real grave, the place he went as his identity faded. That funeral I'd missed was just a transfer of remains from one grave to another. I was suddenly caught with my eyes watering, a surge of something through my body, and a shuddering I could barely quell. As soon as I could, I pulled off the highway, and the first thing to catch my eye was a Journey's End Motel.

My plan had been to go as far as Haileybury today, and it was now only two in the afternoon. Tomorrow was Friday, and I wanted to catch Willy after school and take him and Nan out to dinner. Timmins was a good four hours ahead. If I stopped here, I'd have plenty of driving time, but that was not the problem. I wanted to explore a bit in the TriTown area. But my weariness was not only sudden, it was overwhelming, so I got a room.

The bed was comfortable, but my weariness wasn't, yet, sleepiness, so I just indulged in some ceiling-staring. All those times I had hitch-hiked, there were only two occasions when I had stopped in a motel, because I was generally broke. At the end of the summer of 1953, I'd decided that the Toronto experiment was sufficiently conclusive: I had shown my parents — well, my father — that I was capable of independent living. I'd proved to myself that life as a wage-earner in the big city was solitary, nasty, and long. The drudgery of injecting a thousand mice a day was greater than the satisfaction of displaying cosmopolitan sophistication to my friends on weekends. I was drawn back to the north by the three classic lures of money, sex, and power.

Money was non-existent for me in Toronto. Lab assistants were, I was told, a dime a dozen in Toronto, a phrase which seemed to inform the compensation policy of Connaught Laboratories. Sex was inconceivable in

Toronto without money. I knew no girls there, and to get acquainted would have involved dating, an expensive process. I had read some of Hugh Garner's novels, and I was living on the edge of Cabbagetown, but none of those Garner heroines, tough talking, gum chewing, but honest and true, seemed to be around. The woman on the floor below me was obviously a prostitute, and she scared the daylights out of me. Besides, it wasn't heavy sex that I was after, though I did think about it a lot. It was more being with girls, talking with them, sharing laughs. That happened when I was visiting Haileybury, with old school friends, actually girls of my age still in school.

Power? My independence in Toronto was a sham, my existence a scurrying for cheap food, cheap lodging. Power is choice, I realized, and my Golden Age of choice had been that year of living with Nana, but going my own way. That was what I wanted, more than anything.

So back up north I went in September of 1953. Nana seemed a bit doubtful about us renewing a joint household, but I was prepared to pay (nominally) for the room and board, she was a grandmother, and there didn't seem to be a reason to say no. My parents and Willy were on the edge of another move, this time over to Nipigon over in Northwestern Ontario, and I would have been a complication.

A job was easy to get. A friend of my father ran a small mine out of North Cobalt, the Harrison-Hibbert, known as the Mud Mine for its constant drip of dirty water underground. I was seventeen, but had some documentation saying eighteen, the minimum age for underground work. I started at $1.10 an hour, which worked out better than my wage in Toronto by twenty cents. To keep the perspective on those wages and inflation in Canada, I should point out that a dollar ten would buy eleven draft beer. The last time I bought a draft beer in Parksville, a larger one, to be sure, it cost over two dollars. Also, my pay cheque was an uncomplicated thing, a very little income tax, no CPP, pennies for unemployment insurance. We were a non-union mine, which meant some freedom. The manager didn't care how long we worked, as long as we got a round out, and a certain tonnage out to the mill. On day shift, we tended to work the full eight hours, but on night shift, no manager on site, we would hustle, get a round out and be home before two AM while being paid till three.

It was not all beer and skittles. The work was hard, and I was not. I learned to muck over the foot, using the steel toe of my boot to lever the point of the shovel under the broken rock that would have jarred you if you tried to drive a shovel into it. But I was painfully slow, and a few of my partners made a joke out of it. I watched one of them, at a miners' competition the next year, muck a ton of ore over a four foot screen in a flat eight minutes. That would have taken me almost an hour.

It was my first experience of hard manual labour, and I've smiled ever since when intellectual friends would envy the labourer because he could, they said, think his own thoughts as he worked at his mindless task. It is not mindless. Your whole mind is concentrated on how damned hard it is, and you do not have the energy for elevated thought.

On the home front, my existence was almost idyllic. Nana and I did not rub egos, mainly because we rarely saw each other. Her housekeeper packed my lunchbox for every shift. She said it reminded her of packing lunches for Aurel, her dead husband, whose lunchbox she had packed for thirty years. I made my own breakfast, before Nana got up on my day shift days, well after on my night shift days. Sometimes we had dinner together, but it was almost an arranged thing. I picked up a car, a '32 Graham-Paige coupe, for a hundred dollars. Gas was cheap, and there were contributors for out of town trips, like up to Kirkland Lake in pursuit of interesting girls.

I could have gone on like that for years, maybe becoming fully working class. I was jarred out of it by an accident underground. "Working class" sounds snobbish. It's not. I respected those guys I worked with underground, not just because they earned their money more than I did mine, but because they were fun, they were good to each other, and (mainly) to their families, and they were, except under the influence of, or in search of, alcohol, they were law-abiding. But most of them were not grown up in the sense of being able to make decisions. They had eliminated decision-making from their lives, except for whom to go hunting with. Their hockey loyalties had hardened about age sixteen: about 50% Canadiens, 20% Leafs, 15% Bruins and 15% Red Wings. I never heard a positive comment in the dry (lunchroom) about Rangers or the Black Hawks. Football didn't matter. They played on softball teams, but didn't follow the American game. Basketball was for kids. You talked about hockey, hunting, fishing and drinking.

It's an enticing thought to not grow up into decision making. In the sense that I mean, there were Peter Pans all over the country, felling trees, working in factories, mines, creating our wealth and spending the small share of the wealth that fell to them, without making any decisions except where to go after shift. I might go to Kirkland Lake where there was a girl who might…. My thirty-seven year old partner would go home, play with his kids, make love to his wife, go out with his buddies. Neither of us were making any decisions. I was prepared to opt into this as life. The accident intervened. Nope, sorry, that's a statement of intervention, like Fate, the Divine, the Unconscious, "Id" made me do it. The accident happened. The meaning of accident is that it just happened. But it did make me think about making decisions, about growing up.

The motor hummed along, jerking a little when the tracks shifted left and right. Jim kept his head-lamp straight ahead, angled up a bit to catch the next timber. The timbers were the lowest points. If you kept your head below them, it wasn't going to hit the roof of the drift. Tom's back leaned into his. Maybe Tom was asleep, he often seemed to be just waking up when they stopped near the face.

They were into Agnico property here, going along an old drift to where the Harrison Hibbert was drifting to be able to do exploration back into Harrison Hibbert property. Tom and Jim were drilling and blasting rounds each night, while a day shift crew mucked out the round and laid track to the new face. It wasn't even ore. They would dump it down a chute to an old Agnico stope. It was a long way in to the face, about a mile, and Tom and Jim drove the motor in each night, with the swede machine, steel and powder. He wondered if they were under the lake here. It wasn't much wetter than back at the station, but the water was cleaner.

He slowed before the last turn, easing the handle of the motor back. It looked like the control of a Toronto streetcar, just a handle that meant forward when you pushed it to the left, reverse when you pulled it right. They came around the corner and he slowed to a stop about five feet from the mucking machine. Two shifts, tonight and tomorrow, and they'd be at their target, just widen things a bit for the diamond drill to come in.

The two of them worked swiftly on the setup. The swede drill was hooked to air and water while Jim cleared some muck left at the face. They would drill about twenty-five holes, each seven feet long, into the rock face, load them, and take out the round. Of all the men on shift, they were the farthest out from the station, so their round had to go first. As they went back to the station, other crews, working on raises or stopes, would check them past and light their own rounds. The whole shift was counting on them to finish quickly and bring an early end to the shift.

Jim checked his pocket watch. 7:35 PM. Tom would be wanting to light the round by 1 AM. Jim took a short starter drill, and fitted it into the chuck of the drill. Tom turned on the water, and a spurt came out of the bit. Jim grabbed the steel and set it on the spot Tom indicated. Then Tom fed air to the drill, and Jim struggled to hold the bit on target. The machine worked like a hammer, pounding the steel forward, then back and a quarter turn, then in again, four or five pulses a second, depending on how much air Tom was feeding it, the leg of the drill pushing forward from its own air cylinder. The first couple of inches of each hole were the worst, rock chips and water hitting Jim's face until the bit was far enough in to stay in place.. Jim would get the next piece of steel ready, a five footer, and change steel when Tom told him.The last steel for each hole was over seven feet.

The noise of the machine made talk impossible.Tom made hand signals when he was ready to pull the steel for a change, or to start a new hole. Jim checked the carbide bit as they finished with each steel. They had brought three of each length to make sure the work was uninterrupted.

The first five holes were in the centre of the face, like dots on dice, called the "cut". When they loaded the holes with powder, the centre hole of the cut would be left empty, a space for the explosive force to break into when the other four holes of the cut blasted simultaneously. The rock in a cylinder seven feet long and six inches in diameter would come out as if from a cannon, spraying the drift behind them with small chunks of rock moving at blinding speed.

The next to be drilled were "helpers", holes in a circle about two feet out from the cut. Then shoulder holes, knee holes, top holes and lifters, four holes at the bottom of the face. They would be exploded in a series determined by a timer fuse, and the result would be a fairly clean face, with a pile of muck back near the mucking machine.

The skill of the machine man was not confined to the holding of the drill and steadily forcing the bit into the rock. He also had to "read" the rock, to know exactly where to place each hole so the rock would break in the pattern he wanted, so that the sides of the drift would be vertical, the floor even, the top clean, and the new face even for drilling the next shift. Many times, Jim would be ready to place the starter steel in what seemed to be the obvious place, and Tom would touch his shoulder and indicate a spot a few inches away. Some little crack that Tom could see and he couldn't. Once, he had said "What the hell difference does it make?, only to get a glare from Tom and a real shove at his shoulder to move the damn bit.

The last lifter hole, down at the bottom right of the face was finished at midnight. Jim went back to get the powder box and the fuse set. Each fuse was cut precisely the same length, exactly nine feet for exactly nine minutes of burning before reaching the detonator crimped to one end, the square cut end. Jim picked up a stick of Forcite and rolled it between his palms to loosen it. He handed it to Tom, who opened the paper at one end, slid the detonator and fuse a few inches into the clay-like powder. A sharp twist of the paper, and it was ready for insertion into one of the holes. Tom would slide the Forcite into a hole, then use a long wooden rod to get it to the end, where a few taps of the rod would tamp it firmly. Stick after stick followed it, each tamped with the loading rod. Working together, they got one hole loaded every minute, and then Tom began to attach the timing fuse. This was yellow, in sharp contrast to the black safety fuse, because the timing fuse burned at about two inches a second. Tom hooked it to the protruding ends of the safety fuses so that the four holes of the cut would be lit first, then the helpers, the shoulder and knee holes, and so on. With an enormous "CRUMP", the cut would fire its contents down the drift, then succeeding explosions would collapse the rock into the space left by the cut, breaking it into sizes that the mucking machine could handle. The last holes, the lifters, would throw the muck away from the face. Then everything would be still for hours, allowing the mine ventilation to clear the gases, and the day shift guys would come to clear the muck and lay the track.

As the farthest out, they could light their shot when they wanted. Jim took the swede machine and balanced it on the top of the motor, over the battery compartment. Then he got half the steel. Tom would bring the rest. His watch said ten to one. Pretty good. Why was Tom so slow? He should have had the shot lit and be here by now.

Jim turned to look back towards the face. He was on the seat of the motor, and had to turn around to see anything. His left foot was on the track bed. Tom would be coming down to the left of the mucking machine.

Suddenly, the motor leaped backward. He realized later that the cuff of his oiler jacket had caught the control handle. But now, he couldn't find the handle. His hat and lamp came off, and his left foot was pushed backwards, catching tie after tie on the track, thump, thump, thump. Then a big thump as he hit Tom, and finally a grinding of his left ankle between the motor and the mucking machine. Jim finally got the control handle and shoved it, the motor jumping forward. The Swede drill was in his lap.

Steel was falling. Tom was hopping, holding his knee and cursing. "Stupid little bastard" was the only phrase Jim could make out.

Time, which had seemed to stand still for those moments of violence, must have accelerated during the next few minutes as they tried to sort out the drill, the steel, Jim's hard hat, everything they had brought to the face, Then the thought struck both of them, and Tom voiced it. "The cut!" Later on, Jim, smarting under the accusation of being the stupidest new bug to ever hit the Mud Mine, threw back the accusation that Tom had dawdled at the face after lighting the cut, and that had used up some of their grace time. Now they both concentrated on getting away, getting around the curve of the drift fifty feet away, before the shot went, to hell with the drill and the steel, just get those fragile human bodies out of the way of that cannon shot which would come any second.

They made it, made it by about thirty seconds or so, so it wasn't as close a thing as Jim relived in dreams later. The compression of the shot was still extreme. They were about two hundred yards closer than anyone was supposed to be. But the spray of rock didn't get them, except for a few ricochets that dribbled to their feet. Each of them could have hurt them badly, but not as badly as the main shot, which would have left them bloody scattered pieces.

Later, they sat in the station, the other guys quizzing Tom about the accident, Jim sitting alone and miserable, conscious that his left leg was swelling inside his boot. The air was thick with the smoke from ten cigarettes and two pipes. There was a sharp "pock" from the rock behind. Lalonde looked up. "That's my first." The others continued to talk, but Lalonde and his partner listened intently, counting the explosions. Each explosion arrived first as the "pock" in the wall of the station, sound moving faster through rock than through air. Then the smoke in the station would move a foot or two towards the shaft, then back, with a solemn and strung out "boom" heard through the air. Seven shots. Lalonde stopped his intent listening and lit another cigarette. "All went", he muttered, knowing that meant a clean face tomorrow, no unexploded sticks of Forcite with detonators ready to blow him and McGuire to another life. Like Jim and Tom had almost been blown.

The doctor, Dr. Dunning in Cobalt, who handled all the Compensation cases, looked at the X-ray of Jim's ankle the next day. "Why didn't you break a bone or two? There's about twenty bones in that ankle, and right now they're just floating about. Doubt if you have a tendon left in there. No walking for a month at least, young fella." Jim, whose ankle felt like painful putty ever since they got the boot off last night, thought a month was optimistic. He'd be surprised if he could put weight on that foot for a year. The foot and ankle looked like a case of elephantiasis. Dr. Dunning filled out his section of the Workmen's Comp papers.

"How's Tom's knee?

"Not too bad. He'll be off for two weeks. You're not his favourite person right now. If it were hunting season, I wouldn't go near him."

Nana was sympathetic, she always was. Jim was miserable. Soon the misery began to grind down the sympathy. When he was finally able, three weeks later, to go downtown on crutches, he suspected that Nana was wishing he'd move. Maybe he should.

As it was they came to their decisions simultaneously, but Jim spoke first. "Nana."

"Yes?"

"I was thinking… like maybe I should go back to school."

"In September? Where?"

"No, now. This month. Next week is the first of May, but I bet I could pick up two maths in Grade 13, then get to university in the fall.

Her relief was almost funny in its visibility. She'd been thinking too, and wondering how to break it to him. She wanted to sell the house, move to a small apartment down in Toronto, close to an old friend, who was hoping they could be closer, maybe winter in Florida. If they liked it, they might do it every year. "And I'm still an American citizen, so who knows?"

That surprised him. He'd known she was born in Pennsylvania, but he'd always assumed she'd become a Canadian citizen after marrying Gramp at seventeen. But no, something had held her back.

He started school, taking three math courses: geometry, which he had dropped in the first half of his last year there, trigonometry, and algebra. The same teacher taught all three courses, and he was pretty skeptical about Jim being able to get the credits in the six weeks left before the Departmental exams. But Jim, still on crutches, worked harder that he ever had in school. There was one night, after his ankle healed, when he had to go underground for one shift to round out his compensation time. It was a night of pure terror. When it ended, he tossed the hard hat and lamp down the basement steps and swore never to go underground again. That summer, he helped Nana pack. She sold some furniture, and put some stuff in storage in New Liskeard. The house sold so easily that Jim suspected she head deliberately priced it very low. In early August, his Departmental results came back, three credits, marginal marks but undeniable credits. He got his acceptance at the University of Western Ontario the day after Labour day.

CHAPTER 14

Waking in the motel room in the early evening was disorienting. My neck was cramped from the high foam pillow, and my left ankle had a stabbing pain. Memory is strong.

Growing up is such a complex thing that we can't really assign stages and turning points to the process. Still, I remember the decision to get back to my education vividly. My parents were pleased, of course. Dad had the funds in a trust fund and had been quietly urging me for months to get out of the mine and back to school. On the Easter long weekend, he had been pointed. "Look, Jim, a mine's not right for you. I've worked in one, and it wasn't right for me either, but at the time, I didn't have your options. You've got a good brain, and you can write. I've seen some of the things you did two years back."

Just thinking of that conversation, in the context of what I've written so far in this journal, makes a journalistic correction necessary, not a retraction, but a note about unintended bias. I've been following one strand of my life, one that stretches from that summer of 1949 right through to Dad's death ten years ago. But a life is more a braided rope, with other strands, some involving the same people. I see that I've been giving the impression that Dad and I were daggers drawn year after year, and that's not accurate. In many ways we could get along well. There was just this area of reserve, the feeling that I couldn't be totally open with him, nor him with me. But then, I was already closing down with most people, except Mom.

I got out of the motel to stretch my legs. Walking down O'Brien as far as Scollard Hall felt good. The stars were bright, and there would be frost tonight. Tomorrow, if it stayed clear would be a beautiful drive north, the scarlet maples giving way to the golden poplar and birch. Hunting weather. Nothing was nicer than an old logging road in October, the double 16 gauge under my arm, the leaves in a soggy carpet on the bush floor. And partridge. Although I've lost all urge to hunt, I will never condemn the sport, for I remember the pleasures. I would get going early, 6 AM, and eat at New Liskeard.

As it turned out, I ate at Latchford, because I'd decided to take the turnoff into Cobalt. it had been years since I actually went into the TriTown. In June of '89, when Willy and Nan's oldest girl got married, Dee and I had intended to tour the towns so she could match her mental picture with reality, but we just ran out of time. This time, I phoned Willy from Latchford and told him it might be tomorrow before I got in. I really had to see Cobalt again.

Eleven B is a curvy road. Here was the hill going down to Gillies Lake. Funny, there seems to be a series of Gillies Lakes in Ontario. Had some Scots gamekeeper wandered the province naming lakes? There was one in the middle of Timmins, too. Both it and this one had very muddy bottoms, bush right to the water's edge, very poor swimming. But just up the hill was the road to Bass Lake, and on impulse, I took it.

The road was now paved. In the fifties, it had been washboard, a trial for anyone riding a bike. Over the ONR tracks, i could see the lake and the park, the swim raft on shore of course in this fall season.

Cobalt seemed changed beyond recognition. It was a shock to see the bright, new-looking houses that had been built after the fire that wiped out much of Lang Street in the seventies. The old Lang Street had been a crazy quilt of structures with very few right angles, but now it looked a lot like a town in Southern Ontario. The Wright Sub-division now had its road, Ruby Street, paved, and a cement sidewalk where the old wooden duckboards had been. The pile of waste rock was partly levelled, and the old head frame that had stood right behind our house had disappeared. The pipeline was gone as well. I should have known that, but it seemed strange. Of our old house, there was no trace. It had never had a basement, only a root-cellar. Some trees remained around a rectangle of low scrub that marked where we had lived. Nickel Street showed less change. Our town-owned house had evidently passed into private hands, because there were observable improvements, a glassed in porch, some brick facing, a picture window. I peered up beside it: no wood pile. I'd bet that they had central heating.

I drove the few miles to Haileybury slowly. There was the cemetery, with Mom's body there for almost forty years, Dad's ashes added by Willy. But I wasn't caught unprepared as I had been in North Bay; here, I knew what was around the corner, and I was steeled. But I didn't go in. Maybe on the way back. I had to talk with Willy first, show him what I'd been writing. Haileybury seemed more familiar than Cobalt. Its big fire had been in 1923, a forest fire sweeping in from the northwest and wiping out ninety percent of the town, people standing up to their necks overnight in Lake Temiskaming, waiting for hell to pass over them. It was the rebuilt town that I was familiar with, and it had not changed much in forty years, except for the bypass road coming in the old West Road, and the amalgamation of the liquor and beer stores into a new building near the Matabanick Hotel. The Haileybury Hotel, home of the ten cent draft of hallowed memory, was no more, done in by a fire, and now replaced with a motel.

The Good Food Grill was gone, devoured by time. Buster's, around the corner was still there. I just peeked in, not wanting to know if Buster was still there. I preferred to remember kids dancing to the jukebox, before rock 'n roll, back in my own musical memories. But it was hard to picture now. When I made that decision to go to university, it must have been a real turning. I had visited Haileybury occasionally during university,, but the friends weren't the same, or I wasn't. I remember thinking that they were stuck in some "Happy Days" time warp while I was growing in knowledge and experience, but they were growing too, and it was simply that our shared frame of reference, a few years of parties, some adult-sanctioned, some illicit, drinking (definitely illegal), helter-skelter driving between small towns, and thousand of hours of sitting in restaurant booths or the benches in the pool hall — these things were past, and our presents seemed to need too much explaining. Now I was briefly tempted to call Roger or Bill or Kip, but I knew the probable result: fake delight, embarrassed efforts to arrange a meeting, silence if it happened.

Or maybe I could phone Tom, my partner underground that night I'd racked both of us up. He lived in Haileybury, if he lived at all. He would be over seventy now. No, he was probably still mad.

I'd considered driving out to the Harrison-Hibbert when I came through North Cobalt. It would have been pointless. The mine itself would have been closed by the sixties, if it lasted that long, the head frame would be gone and only a square of fence would mark the shaft. My memories of the place were of shining wet rock, pipes, rails, a constant dripping, and dark holes leading off from the stations.

But I'd found one element of manhood that year. I'd never learned to work as hard and efficiently as those men, but I had learned that complaining didn't make the work go faster, go better, or go away. That, and the notion that you did what you could for the day, there'd be plenty of work to do the next day, and so it would go on. In journalism, I knew lots of people who sought closure, tried to get the story tied nailed down once and forever. They never understood what I meant by "digging" a story, because they had never mined.

But, I reflected as I drove out Lakeshore Road towards New Liskeard, Haileybury was never a mining town. Most of the money had come from mining, but only the south (French) end had worked in the dark and the drips. Eight months of underground work had not made a miner out of me. Dee's parents were farmers, and I had liked them and tried to understand them, but I will never really know what it is to be a farmer. Different from mining, for sure (as Lalonde would say) but how different and in what ways is a mystery to me. I just tried to simplify the surfaces of things for my readers. Quoth Pilate, "What is truth?" Poor bugger never knew how his little quip would echo down the centuries.

I lunched very late, fast food, fries, , almost as if I had worked physically in fact, not just memory. I had told Willy tomorrow, and now I was going to stay in another motel. I drove well past the turnoff for Kirkland Lake, and stopped at Matheson. I had to get out of Cobalt and Haileybury. The last time I had spent a night there was in a motel, really a group of cabins, in North Cobalt, the weekend we buried my mother.

Jack was shaking me. "Jim, wake up. No, wake up. It's your brother on the phone and he says it's important." Jack's room was closest to the phone, and if it wouldn't stop ringing in the small hours, he would have to answer it. I swung my legs out and made contact with the floor. That always sends the message to my brain that there's no backsliding, wakefulness has to take over,

It was Willy, and his voice was high, squeaky, as if his throat was tightened up. "Jim?"

"Yeah, what is it? God, it's almost 4 AM!"

"Jim, Mom's dead. About three hours ago. She came in from that reading club, and she had a headache. Then…" His voice couldn't keep going, and Jim only heard a series of gasping noises.

"Willy! Willy! You OK?"

"I … guess so. But Mom…"

"Is Dad there?"

"He is, but I don't think he can talk. Uncle Jim's here." Dad was in North Bay again this April of 1956. Jim Gardner was still in Cobalt, which was just switching over to an OPP detachment. He must have been the first person Dad called. Or Willy. Jim wondered where he himself had been at 12:30, 1 AM. Just leaving the Ceeps after a few beers. That was when Mom was dying.

Uncle Jim's deep bass voice came on. "Jimmy?"

"Yes, sir.

"Jimmy, I'm so sorry. There was no real warning. There was probably no pain, the doctor said, except that headache. A stroke, they think."

"How's Willy? And Dad?"

"OK, all things considered. Can you get up here?"

"Yeah, I'll have to get the car from Norm." Another guy and Jim were partners in a '36 Plymouth, which they had bought for $175 two months before. Norm kept it most weekdays, since he lived north of London, past the bus routes, while Jim had it mostly on weekends. "I should get away by 8:30. Be in the Bay mid-afternoon." Tuesday: Norm had a nine o'clock class, but he would come early, and Jim could get the car at the University. He'd go north, then swing east to Mitchell, work his way to 27, then north to Barrie to join 11.

"Good. The funeral will probably be Friday, in Cobalt. I'm going back there in an hour or two, so I won't see you when you get here. I'll make arrangements with Father Duffy. Probably, your Dad will want to go up tomorrow with the… I can get you all a place to stay.I just have to phone someone."

"Thanks, Uncle Jim."

"The least I can do. She was a wonderful lady."

Then Willy came back on, and Jim tried soothing him. "I'll be there as soon as I can. Take care of Dad, eh?"

He cooked up some tired hamburger and an egg in the kitchen of the frat house. Mom was dead. He felt it had to be some stupid mistake, a medical error of some kind that he'd have to sort out when he got up there. How could Willy know for sure? But Uncle Jim had acted like it was real. No need to pack, most of his stuff was in a trunk in North Bay anyway. Exams started in three weeks, less really, 20 days. Why now? in a month, he would have been home, able to take care of her, stop this thing.

There was light in the east as he walked up Richmond. A bus went past, tires hissing, and pulled in to a stop half a block ahead. He didn't try for it, his legs wouldn't respond. Anyway, there was piles of time. He'd phone Norm from the U, get him in as early as possible. Better, there was a phone at St. Joe's, the booth outside the Emergency. Six-thirty now, give or take five minutes, he could still tell time without a watch, even if the universe foundations were shaking. Then he'd just keep on walking, meet Norm at the gates, drop him at the Arts building, and take off. There was an all night gas station up by Highway 7 where he could fill up. He had sixteen dollars in his pocket, enough to get him to North Bay. He could cash a cheque there.

In the car, Norm was embarrassed, inarticulate. "Gee, Jim, that's ... awful. Did ..." Did what, Norm? Did she say anything, just before? Did she know what was happening? Did I act like a good son, like you are, Norm, you and your mother up on that farm? Did what?

"Gotta get going, Norm. OK to drop you here?" It was the cafeteria, an old army H-hut structure. It was open, lights on, and a bunch of students heading in for breakfast. Jim was hungry again, but he wasn't going to stop. Norm got out, but held the door of the old Plymouth open while he struggled again for words.

"You, um, gonna be OK? I mean, do you want ...?"

"I'll be fine. Sorry about the car. I won't be back till next week, maybe a week from tomorrow."

"That's all right. I'll get a ride from my ..." Norm struggled to find a way out of it, but finally had to say the word. "... mother." Then he got the door closed, and Jim was alone.

He stopped for some food around eleven, just coming into Barrie on 27. The news was on a radio in the diner. A company of paratroops, Royal Canadian Regiment, had been dropped miles from their drop zone on a training jump, and the hundred or so men landed in and around Preston, a little town near Galt. Jim was taking officer training through the COTC and knew a few regular force types, though nobody in 1 RCR. He imagined the men seeing the downtown of Preston rushing up at them, power lines, three and four story buildings, bridges. They had probably tried desperately to side slip by spilling air, increasing their drop speed. The radio reported that there were no confirmed dead, but dozens of injuries, many of them serious. Meanwhile, the planes would have droned on, the pilots unconscious having made a tragic mistake.

The image wouldn't leave his mind as he drove north on Highway 11. The car was slow at first, and positively rheumatic going up hills. No compression to speak of, pistons just slapping back and forth in the cylinders. Maybe he'd get a ring job, have it done in North bay. Dad knew some guys who ran a garage there. Dad. How come he hadn't talked with him, why had it been left to Willy, poor kid, and Uncle Jim? He felt his neck reddening with anger. He and Willy had just been dropped like those soldiers, no look at where they were landing. He'd been basically all right, going to Western, and older anyway, twenty now, but Willy had been to three schools in the past four years as the OPP moved Dad around. Poor Mom, too, all those moves, going into apartment after apartment, no garden. This move to North Bay was supposed to be good for four or five years, a long posting, and Mom was going to be looking for a house with a good sized yard, she'd said in her letter.

Now there'd be no more letters. If he could only write one now, it would be the really long one he'd never gotten around to. He'd send her things, things she probably missed. The car began to slow on a long hill, and he thought about that kids' story, the little engine that could or something. Why couldn't he ever carry through on the things he determined to do? Over the crest, down to forty, then picking up speed on the downslope. Dad again. He had to take some of the blame, maybe a lot. He hardly saw the road, getting sad again, then mad, but decided to stop at South River for coffee. Almost four, and another hour to go.

The radio in Happy Landing was on about those soldiers dropping into Preston. Some had been dragged across roofs, then swung into buildings across the street. That was the trouble with jumping, a sergeant in Borden had told him. Everything's supposed to be flat, predictable, the jumpmaster doesn't make mistakes, and as for the Air Force, they are just perfect in their navigation. Until you're out of the plane, and the chute snaps you like the end of a whip, and you look down and there's every damned hazard you can think of, coming up at you.

As he got back into the car, he knew that he was committed, he was going to be in the Bay in an hour, and the situation there was a total mystery to him.

CHAPTER 15

Willy, as usual, saved the day when I arrived at the North Bay apartment on that sunny April afternoon in 1956. His misery was so total that I couldn't keep thinking of my own resentment. I could not move without him following me, first with wide eyes, and then with his gangling fourteen year old body. I had to shut the bathroom door in his face twice, and he was there, helplessly waiting when I emerged.

The fridge had been foraged over by Dad and Willy, probably without either of them thinking what they were doing or eating. I opened it and realized that everything there had been bought by Mom, that she had plans, never divulged to the others, for every bit of food there, and we would never know what the plans were. The doorbell went while I was looking in the fridge, then again. Willy was sitting at the kitchen table, fixing me with a stricken stare. I went into the living room. Dad just sat there, his face frozen as the doorbell rang a third time. It was a woman who lived downstairs, holding a casserole with oven mitts. She murmured something and thrust it at me. I held it, my hands hurting from the heat and stared at her. "Uh, thanks, Mrs. … ?"

"Renwick. Downstairs. Really sorry. She was nice."

She was gone. Her prayer for the dead was still burning my hands, and I turned to put it down on the little telephone table, bumping Willy, who had moved up to a within a few inches of my back. I found some potholders in the kitchen and brought the dish into the kitchen, putting it on the table. Knives, forks, plates, milk, and it was done, dinner. I sat Willy on a chair and told him to stay right there.

"Dad? Dinner's on the table. Mrs. Renwick brought it up." I should have lifted the lid; he might ask what it was, and I had no idea. But he just stared. I touched his shoulder and he shook violently, but his eyes did turn to me. "Dad? Come and eat." He got up obediently and went into the kitchen. I said grace, and all of us followed the movements, the sign of the cross, head down, another sign of the cross. I got up for a serving spoon, and finally opened the casserole lid. It was a stew. I never saw Mrs. Renwick again, and certainly never will, for she was over fifty then, thirty-eight years ago. Wherever she has gone to, I hope she knows that we were more grateful than my clumsy note, left inside the washed casserole dish outside her door the next morning, expressed. Or I was grateful. Willy was filled with so much pain that other feelings had no room. Dad was in some other world.

We drove north in the morning. Uncle Jim had called about 9 PM to say that we would be staying at the Kerwins' house, who were out of town but had entrusted the keys to him. He had asked them by phone if we could use the house. I drove Dad's car, a '54 Plymouth auctioned out of police service. At every stage. I had to practically point him and then start him moving.

And that is how it went right up to Friday, the day of the funeral. Dad would finally murmur some reply to people who talked to him, but the look of lacerated pain he gave them made even the most sympathetic back away instinctively. I began to feel that resentment again. Dammit, I thought, I'm feeling pain too, but I've got to talk to all the people in Cobalt and Haileybury. I couldn't blame Willy for his incapacity, but I did blame Dad. On Thursday night, Uncle Jim held a wake at his house. I got Willy home about eleven, and into bed, then went back so people would see I wasn't deserting dad. Got him home and bedded down around one. The Kerwins' house was a two bedroom, so I was on the living room couch.

I was just dropping off, when Dad got up and wanted to talk. About Mom. He was crying, and everything he said sounded maudlin. I loved him, and I was annoyed with him, and mainly I was totally bushed. My vision was blurring with fatigue. He would say something and then look at me intently. Most times, I didn't really hear him, just nodded and hummed something in reply. That seemed to satisfy him. Maybe we were both a little drunk. He had been gulping down drinks with a desperate jerkiness. I looked at the clock on the Kerwins' mantle. Almost three. I went into the kitchen and poured him about four ounces of rye in a tumbler. He drained it, coughed, and started to talk again. The funeral was scheduled for ten in the morning. I stood up and touched his shoulder. That worked. He got up, and I led him to bed.

Now, thirty-eight years later, as I looked at the dirty ceiling of the Matheson motel room,I thought about waking up in the Kerwins' living room that Friday morning. It was eight o'clock, and it was damn lucky I had a built in alarm. I chivvied Willy and Dad from their beds, organized their toothbrushing and Dad's shaving, fed them some cereal, got them dressed and out of the house. St. Patrick's was only two blocks away, but we took the car because it would be part of the cortege. Dad had frozen his face into impassivity again, but Willy was beginning to emerge from his state of shock.

I've been to a lot of funerals, often for friends, but even more often to efforts to eulogize the great, the near-great, and the so-so's whose survivors wanted the world to think great, so much so that journalists were invited as a matter of course. My Mom's funeral was one of the few in which the gathering was united in genuine mourning. Everyone in the church knew her personally, and it seemed that the whole of Cobalt and half of Haileybury crowded that little church on the corner. Father Duffy, flawless in the Latin prayers of the mass and in those parts of the funeral service in the vernacular, proved almost aphasic when it came to his own composition. He paused, groped, mispronounced, and placed his emphasis randomly. He could have been an alien visitor to earth, flipping through a phrasebook to communicate. Yet he did communicate the essential: sorrow and amazement that this woman, barely thirty-eight, a woman everyone respected and, yes, loved, was gone.

Sitting in the diner over breakfast in Matheson, my feet soaked from the three inches of snow that had fallen, I thought about that eulogy. I remembered sitting in the front pew, dizzy with fatigue and emotion. At moments during the funeral I felt a great communion with all those people in the church, a sense of being totally at one with them. But in the intervening years, I have seen only a few of them, and I doubt that I could recognize even them with the sureness I could recognize Mrs. Renwick.

I took my time with coffee, and even watched some TV in the motel room before leaving. There was no rush to get to Timmins, and I'd lunch in South End so as to arrive after the lunch hour at Willy's. It was Saturday now, let them relax from the week.

Matheson is a farm community, little more than a wide spot on the road. It is part of the Great Clay Belt, touted before the First War as a rival to the breadbasket of the prairies. Many homesteaders broke their spirits on the land and their ploughs on the clay. Matheson was burned out in a forest fire around 1916 with more dead than most communities that had the same disaster. Wheat never worked in Northern Ontario.

A few miles north of Matheson, Highway 101 strikes west into the Porcupine. Over eighty years ago, prospectors paddled through the meandering weed choked rivers, through clouds of mosquitos and black flies, and some of them struck richness: Sandy McIntyre, Benny Hollinger, and their mines started a stream of gold pouring towards the centres of finance, a flow that continues to this day. The road was clear of snow, but wet and shiny, with a little ridge of grey slush on each side that would grow during the coming months to huge ridges blocking the view to each side of the road.

After the funeral in St. Patrick's, after the interment, we had gone back to the house, then out to eat at another family's house, their name lost to me now, though I remember it was on Galena Street. Dad seemed to be coming to life, and Willy relaxed under the maternal glow of Aunt Rita, Uncle Jim's wife. I was getting more and more itchy, fatigue and jumpiness working together. Finally, about eleven, we went back to the Kerwins'. Dad gave me a bi.g hug and went off to bed. Willy collapsed. Hugging me, not talking, and here I'd been carrying the load of the last three days. I stretched out and tried to sleep in the warmth of grievance, but the sleep was restless. There was a twin bed beside Willy, but I thought I had to be available, and I hated the thought that I had to be.

The next morning, the second last Saturday in that April, brought some improvement in my mood. I tried to think of Mom, and found that grief is hard to sustain. It feeds itself, but you can't call it up at will. I could be efficient, and I was in matters of food and clothing, directing my two charges. Dad had regressed since the night before, become morose rather than sad, bitter. Uncle Jim came around, and the two of them talked in the living room. I grabbed Willy, and we walked downtown. We were stopped by at least a dozen people who wanted to tell us how beautiful the service had been, nice people who seemed to be backing me into a hot and sticky corner. At five, we went back to find about twelve casseroles and a sleepy father who had been given quite a bit of rye as an anti-depressant. We ate a sampling. Then I knew I had to get out, that if I stayed in the house, I would lose balance. I walked three blocks to the taxi downtown, and went to Haileybury.

I drank a lot that night. Some friends felt real sympathy, but their social skills were limited to buying me beer. An alcoholic blackout is a scary thing: it's not just a fuzzy memory, it's a period when you are there, you are acting out things, but you are not aware.

Now I had crossed the Frederickhouse River, and was getting close to the Kidd Creek Metallurgical Site. The plume of steam rose ahead of me. Very soon I'd have to talk with Willy, and at some point I'd have to get to the nub of the matter. Ten years ago, after Dad's death, the real death, not the Alzheimer death, Willy had asked, gently, about what happened the weekend of Mom's funeral. I had brushed the question aside as not relevant. But I did not know whether it was relevant or not, because I did not know then, nor do I know now, what happened. All I know is that Willy woke me on that Sunday morning, and I couldn't open my left eye.

"Jim! Wake up, Jim!"

He was prodding Jim's right shoulder. Jim turned away from him on the sofa, and his left cheek brushed the fabric of the upholstery. It stung, and he pushed himself up.

"What happened? Who hit you?"

"Where's Dad?"

"There's a note in the kitchen. He's gone over to the church."

"What time is it?" For once, his ability to tell the time without a watch or a clock was gone. It was light out, that was all he knew.

"Half past eight. But the first mass is at nine, and he's been gone … I don't know how long."

Jim touched the left side of his face. His eye was swollen shut. Suddenly, he felt nauseated, and he got up, moving quickly to the washroom off the kitchen. He tried to be sick, retching, considering putting a finger down his throat, but there was nothing there. His face in the mirror was a mess, eye shut, swelling over the cheekbone, flesh turning a brownish yellow with a red flush around the swelling. He opened his mouth experimentally, moving his jaw left and right. That was all right. Was it possible he'd gotten in a fight? He remembered being in a cabin in North Cobalt, in someone's room. Before that, the beverage room in Haileybury with Ken and Bill and … some other guys.

Then he knew whose room. It was a guy he'd worked with at the Harrison-Hibbert, Rheal some-body, who was in town off the drills, having his bash before going back into the bush for another three months. There'd been ten or fifteen bottles on the old bureau. Ken had been there too. The last thing he could remember was looking at Rheal passed out on the bed, and Ken saying something about a taxi.

He checked his wallet. He'd spent maybe fifteen, sixteen dollars, and he hadn't been rolled. He must have gotten down to Cobalt somehow. Would the police have brought him home? Possible, they'd know about Mom and the funeral. Or maybe he'd hired a taxi. But nothing about that motel room had the message of fight in it. All three had been drunk, but nobody was mad. At one another, anyway.

His own anger about Dad, about the weight that had been shoved on him the past week, about the unfairness of Mom's death, all that resentment had boiled up early in the evening. He remembered telling Ken and Bill, and someone else — not Rheal, he had come in later — about how his father had just gone to pieces, but would never admit anything was his fault, and some other stuff too, even going back to Gramp and that funeral.

he splashed some water on his face, then patted it as gently as he could with the towel. When he came out of the washroom, Willy was at the kitchen table, holding Dad's note. Jim took it from him. "Gone to church to pray. For Mom, for me. Jim, I'm so terribly sorry."

Beside the sink was an empty rye bottle and another three quarters full. Somebody had drunk a good twenty ounces of rye since supper the night before. "Willy, did anybody come to visit last night?"

"No. Unless later. I went to bed about nine. I was really tired."

"Was Dad drinking before you went to bed?"

"Yeah, some. He's really sad, you know, Jim."

"I know. We all are, aren't we? How are you feeling now?"

"Just kinda … not there. Not as bad as before the funeral. Jim, did you get in some kind of a fight with Dad?"

"I'm not sure. Yeah, I guess I must have. I don't know what about though. Maybe I said something he took the wrong way."

"Coming to mass? It's time."

"No, not like this. You go ahead. I might go to eleven." He might not, too. The past year, at university, he'd really gotten out of the habit. Before that, even. Two years before, before that accident in the mine, he'd started to skip mass, go uptown at the right time to keep Nana happy, then sit in the Good Food Grill for an hour with a coffee before going home. Suddenly he recalled his thoughts during the funeral mass, that he was going to start going to mass regularly, offer that up for Mom, do something he knew she wanted. But right now, the way he was feeling, the way he looked, not this week.

Willy went. He made some toast and thought about brewing some coffee, but he didn't know where the Kerwins kept everything. He went into the room that he supposedly shared with Willy, though he'd hardly slept in it. He got some fresh clothes out of his suitcase, then shoved his dirty ones into it; he had a feeling he'd be heading south today.

Leaving the Kerwins' house, he went west a block first, and then along the alley running parallel to the highway. Going past the church didn't seem like a good idea. Sunday morning was pretty quiet, of course. Buses didn't start running till noon. He had about a six block walk to downtown, and he saw only about four cars in that time, all people going to church, one heading to Haileybury where there was a Pentecostal Assembly. He sat for a while on the steps going up from the Fraser House to the High School.

When he got back to the house, it was after noon. The meeting with Dad was anti-climactic. For hours he'd been rehearsing several possibilities ranging from an abject apology from himself (for what, for God's sake?) to a dignified granting of forgiveness. But he had made up his mind that he was heading south. He'd catch the six PM train to North Bay.

Dad was sitting on the sofa. He got up, came over to Jim, and put his arms around him. Jim said, "I'm sorry, dad. I guess I must have made you unhappy."

"No, my fault. We should have talked, you were right. But I just couldn't. And when you said those things, something snapped. How's your eye? Let me look." His fingers were gentle. "I think it'll be all right. Does it hurt when I press there?" There was a bit of pain, not much. Jim said it was OK, nothing broken.

What had he said, what were "those things"? He waited for Dad to carry on, but he didn't. A lunch sat on the table, sandwiches made by some neighbour. dad said something about the sermon, some malapropism of Father Duffy's, and Jim just smiled and nodded. It didn't seem to matter that he hadn't gone to mass. All of that was in the past, a past he was going to cut away from.

And he was not surprised when Dad said they were going to drive to North Bay that afternoon. "We've got to get back to some routine." Willy looked grave, Jim decided to concur.

"Yeah, exams start in a couple of weeks, and I've got a paper due on Tuesday, and … I know Mom would want us all to get on." Nothing more was said, Dad putting on a forced cheerfulness, and

Jim responding. Willy seemed mystified. Dad drove the hundred miles because Jim's distance judgment was not good.

He slept over in the Bay. Everyone was politely cheerful. The old Plymouth would make it to London. Time to get back to the tasks.

CHAPTER 16

Porcupine, South Porcupine, then the few miles of bush — except for the cemetery, why did they always put cemeteries along the highways in the north? — and I was driving down into Schumacher. They've changed the road here, putting a wide road along the old railway right of way and making it skirt the hills and curves of Schumacher. I swung left, taking the old, slow way through. Schumacher and Cobalt always seem related in my mind, the same sort of genial disregard of building codes, maybe even of carpenters' squares. Cobalt, the old Cobalt before that fire, looked like something built by a hyperactive kid with thousands of coloured blocks. Schumacher was the same, false-fronted hotels, huge rooming houses, with the big red head frame of the McIntyre looming up over the little lake.

Then into Timmins proper, just over two hills. Willy's house is out in the west, in an area called Melrose, down on the flats beside the Mattagami River. I drove through the downtown, along Algonquin. There was a little strip of snow, already grey with water, along the curbs. After turning up Theriault Boulevard and past the houses, up by the two big schools, I saw snow on the soccer fields. Left again, following the airport signs. Lunch time. There was a roadhouse down in a little plaza across from the river where Willy and I had gone for a beer the last time I was here. There it was. Saturday noon, it shouldn't be crowded.

I had a big bowl of wonton soup, full of fat noodles. It seemed to be an odd time to be questioning, here at the end of a two thousand mile journey, but why had I come? Gloria Peet was dead, Gramp, Mom, Dad, all in that order. Why disturb things, why cut into that ice buildup again to find and then dissect the corpses that were resting, suspended, all questions frozen? More than that, what right did I have to force this thing on Willy?

Someone with less experience of writer's block than I have might have turned back here, within a few blocks of Willy's house. I recognized all the symptoms of backing away from commitment. Once words are on the page, they assume an identity outside yours, and changing their patterns is hard to do. So it's simplest to let your thoughts swirl around unanchored to paper or even to little patterns of bytes in a memory. But eventually one has to freeze the thoughts into a pattern that means something and put it down in all its imperfection. I remember some English teacher — must have been the Scots lady in Haileybury — who quoted a French novelist, Flaubert, I think, to the effect that he had spent a whole morning agonizing about putting a comma in a particular phrase, then the whole afternoon coming to the conclusion that the comma had to come out. She was trying to prove the value of tight editing, but I was iconoclast enough to point to Flaubert's vast output and calculate that he would have had to live to nine hundred to write it at the rate she described.

What I was going to have to commit to Willy was some range of experience of which he would only have part awareness, something I myself didn't understand except that it started with Gloria Peet and was tied to Gramp and Dad and to Dad and me. Armed with this resolve, if it can be called that, I pulled into their driveway.

It's always a shock to see my kid brother is middle aged. Every time we part, I seem to start a process of subtracting years from him, usually ending up with him looking about thirty-five. But he is fifty-three, turned fifty-three a week before my arrival, and while he looks healthy, he hasn't found any fountain of youth, except in his grin. That has never aged. He was grinning as he hugged me, as he pulled me through the door, as Nan and I exchanged a gentler hug. He wanted to feed me and I declined. Nan just watched us with amused interest. I knew if I agreed to eat, she would have gone into the kitchen and worked wonders, but until the decision was made, she wasn't going to fash herself.

Their house had always looked like a multi-compartmented rumpus room, and the fact that their youngest, my niece Gail, was in her freshman year at York, and they were empty-nesters, at least until Christmas, did not affect the genial disorder. There was a pile of student projects on the coffee table. Willy taught Grades Seven and Eight, usually, except for a couple of years when he had been on special assignment as a consultant developing curriculum. He always referred to that as his "unreal" period. I knew that he had been offered a place on the principal's course a couple of times, but he declined, as he put it, to institutionalize unreality. Now he was "coasting" to retirement, which meant that his work week was curving down to about forty-eight hours, and he was actually taking some summers off. In four years, he was going to pull the plug.

"This your first snow?"

"Almost Hallowe'en? Look Jim, you know Northern Ontario better than that. We had a fair bit two weeks ago, but there's been a few warm days and it all went. This stuff will stay, I'm pretty sure, and we'll be in the deep freeze for at least four and a half months. How's the weather on Vancouver Island? I'm sure you're dying to tell us."

This was one of our standing jokes, and I fell in with it. Then we talked about their kids, and about Laura and Ken. "That Laura," he said, "she must have gotten that wicked sense of humour from Dee. She sent us a letter last month, a sendup of school opening. I changed a few names in it and used it in my class." Did I look surprised that Laura was writing to her uncle? I thought back to August, the month I was stalled in this narrative, just spiralling from past to present to past. I'd been wondering how long she and Vic could stay when they visited. Then she called about Vic's reassignment, and how it meant no trip to the Island this year. I remember being offhand about it: probably just as well, I was all tied up with a project, no, not really a freelance assignment, how's the weather in Edmonton.

Willy had said something. "What?"

"Oh, I meant not like Dee exactly. Sorry, Jim, I guess things still hurt a lot, don't they?" I nodded, and concentrated on the burning itch behind my eyes. He went on. "It's like our kids. I can see Mom in Robyn, Nan too, but definitely Mom. Al has a lot of you, Grant is sort of like Dad, at least in mannerisms and voice. But Gail, I wonder, well, who is that coming back in her? And Laura's the same. Which part of our ancestry, I wonder, and then I realize it's her being herself, that maybe with humans there's such a thing as a totally new being."

"Come on, Willy. Of all people … you teachers are supposed to hold that uniqueness of kids sacred. You talk about it enough."

"Unique, definitely. But you know, at a parents' night, some parent I've never met before, I can usually guess which kid, and not from looks either. The way they talk, the way they sit, the way they look at each other before one speaks. And sometimes when I meet the aunt or uncle of a student ... it shows, Jim, nothing more than that."

I was ready to let Willy call the turns of the conversation as long as he wanted. But he had been a teacher for a long time, and he can tell when someone in the class is encouraging digression. "Jim, you didn't come all the way from Lotusland to talk about how the kids are doing. What's going on?"

"It's not easy to start, Willy." Nan had gone to the kitchen, and I could hear coffee perking. "Can we go for a walk in a few minutes, and I'll give you an outline of the problem. Then I've got some stuff for you to read. Most of it is printed out, but I have to get to a printer to get the rest off my laptop."

"This is sounding like a legal case or something. Only the documents count, eh? OK on the walk, but tell me one thing first — are you getting involved with a woman? Is that the mystery?"

I almost laughed. Gloria Peet and I were involved, all right. "Not a live one, Willy. Can we save it for the walk?"

After coffee, out we went, Willy lending me some bush boots. We're the same size, and they felt comfortable. He didn't appear to make any signals to Nan, but she seemed to know that we had some brother to brother stuff to get cleared. He gave her an impulsive hug at the door, and she glowed. My brother is a very lucky man.

We walked the three blocks to the highway that goes out to the airport, and turned left. After a few hundred yards, the highway and the river come close together. The Mattagami — not a wide river, but a fast one — flowed north here on its way to James Bay. First it would meet another river, the Abitibi I thought, and then eventually this water would be a trickle in the mighty flow of the Moose River, miles wide. The water here was dark grey, almost purplish, and I could see snags on the far shore, trees and branches caught against the muddy bank. In a few weeks, the banks would be thick with ice, the river rushing even faster in the constriction. Eventually it would be skinned over, and there would be a peaceful surface, with only the odd spot, usually at a bend, where turbulence kept it from freezing. Underneath, this black water would keep pushing north, now encased in a huge pipeline of ice and frozen mud.

In the spring there would be floods up north. These rivers would thaw down here, close to the Arctic Watershed, while they were still firmly frozen farther north. The rivers would rise in their banks with the spring runoff, and send recalcitrant blocks of ice swirling north to meet the immovable ice close to James Bay. The chunks would pile up, freeze together in the icy April nights, and form huge dams. Floods sixty feet above normal river levels were not uncommon. I talked to Willy about this, and he nodded, though he knew the north better than I did.

Finally: "Jim, you finished with the hydrographics? Or is this some metaphor?"

It was, though I hadn't intended it that way. Maybe there are Freudian digressions as well as Freudian slips. "You're expecting this to come out in a flood, Willy?"

"Not exactly. But when you run over at the mouth, it's usually because you're having a hard time starting on what you really want to say." We had stopped. It was about 4:30, and the sun was reddening and swelling as it neared the line of bush on the west side of the Mattagami.

"Did you ever hear the name Gloria Peet?"

"Somewhere ... a long time ago. Hey, wasn't that the name of the girl who ... the one you found in a mine way back?"

"That's what we figured her name was. But I found out a few months ago that Gloria Peet lived until this year, just died in May in Toronto."

"Is this journalism, Jim? You're retired, and surely that kind of story... " He didn't want to say anything about tabloids. Willy always followed my writing, and every time I did a story for *Macleans* or the *Globe*, I knew its publication would be followed swiftly by a letter from my brother.

"No, it's personal. The story that she'd died started up ... more like it turned on some tap of memory, and it's got me worried. About Dad, and Gramp, and Evvy. Do you remember that name?'

"Wasn't that Dad's sister? The one who ran away to Vancouver or something?"

"Yes, and she wrote back that she was OK, but there was something ... I mean, Dad didn't seem to believe she was OK, or even in Vancouver." The impossibility of communicating what I didn't even know loomed up. A huge dark bank of cloud rolled north and swallowed the red sun. I shivered. "You cold?"

"A bit. Do you want to head back?"

"Not right away. Look, let's go to that pub down the road." At this moment, the place seemed inviting. Before I'd started this revelation. We walked that way, crossing oer to get to the east side of the highway. Cars coming along swung out to avoid splashing us, but a truck coming south, way over on the far side, sent up a curtain of grey slush that coated my whole right side.

Willy brushed at the slush on my raincoat. "Miss Vancouver Island yet, Jim?"

"Yes. Water is a helluva lot nicer when it stays in one form and in its place. But it is good to be here with you and Nan."

We sat in the pub, in a dark brown booth along the front windows. A tall man was sitting at the bar, hunched over in a cloud of cigarette smoke. I remembered him from my lunch stop. He waved at Willy, and Willy waved back. "One of the high school teachers," he said. "Now what the hell is this all about, Jim?"

And so I told him. No conclusions, for I hadn't reached any yet that my journalistic conscience would allow open expression, but a summary of these pages. He listened, didn't question, except to say, "You've got this written down, you say?"

"Yes, except I have to get the last bits printed out."

"From your laptop. DOS?"

"Yes, WordPerfect 5.1"

"Want to do it right now?"

I didn't really, but I could hardly say that. I nodded and he got up and went over to the tall man at the bar. I watched them, and suddenly I wanted a cigarette, an urge I hadn't felt for years. Then they were coming back to the booth. "Fred, this is my brother, Jim. Fred Guest." We shook hands. His hand was huge. "Fred will help us on the printout, up at the school. He'll give us a ride to pick up your laptop."

We each had some beer to finish, and Fred didn't have any, so I ordered one for him. He looked a little aggrieved, so I amended the order to three beers. I hurried to make sure we all finished at the same time, a time to drink, a time to go, to everything there is a season. Then we were climbing into an incredibly messy pickup truck. Fred, if his consumption since noon had been anything like the way he put down the last beer, must have been drunk, but Willy seemed unworried.

In less than an hour, I had the printout. I had worried about Fred looking at it, but he didn't seem interested. As the printer churned out the pages, he asked me about journalism, and I was surprised at his lucidity and his knowledge of writing in Canada. But he was drunk. When he dropped us back at Willy's house, Willy suggested that he come in for coffee, maybe stay to dinner. "No, I'll get something back at the pub." I thanked him, and he was off.

Dinner was a pleasant interlude. Nan had the capacity to spread a circle of calm about herself, nothing hurried, nothing late. Willy made no reference to our conversation. We ate a pot roast which seemed to come from some beef heaven, the sort of fate an animal might be willing to die for. It was years since I had pot roast. Dee, while a perfect wife for me, had never really enjoyed cooking, and since her death, eating was just something I had to do from time to time. And no restaurant will ever put pot roast on your plate right from the pot; they seem to have to dry it out for a while in some special chamber so that the fibres become little toothpicks.

I gave Willy the manuscript to put on top of the printout from the school. "Tonight?" he said, eying the pile of paper.

"Only as fast as you want."

"You know, I've got some stuff downstairs from that time. Stuff from Nana's house, remember, when she gave up the storage in New Liskeard. And some from Dad's trunk, after he died. But you looked at that then. Remember, you sent that suitcase up here when you and… when you and Dee moved west."

"I'd like to look at it again. I had a mind-fix then."

I went with him to the basement, where it took some shifting of boxes. The butter box was still the same as the last time I saw it, when I put Gramp's files in it. Dad's papers were no longer in the suitcase I had sent up to Timmins. Willy explained that with four kids going off to university, there had been a constant shuffling of luggage. Finally, he found a box labelled "Martini Rossi" with, in black marker on the side, "Dad's papers".

"Just so I'm not the only one doing a lot of reading." We lugged the two boxes to the rec room. "No hockey tonight." I put on a suitably mournful expression, for I had found that you do not kid a hockey fan about the players' strike. Even if you had been kidded about the baseball strike. I would put my life in Willy's hands with full confidence, but I couldn't kid him about hockey. I think sports must occupy a lower — no, not lower, not atavistic either, but a level in ourselves that gets fixed around age twelve, and the reactions come from that kid within. Is that so much different from my Russian Doll conceit? Maybe it is. Willy can reach himself in there, and I can't reach myself. He can feel the crunch of a check, hear the boom of his body slamming into the boards, feel the sting of ice on his face. I never played hockey, nothing organized anyway, because I was so small all those years. High school basketball, back in the fifties anyway, did not have the same bonding potential.

He looked at the two boxes. "I've never gone through them, you know. After Mom died, Dad was different. Not angry or anything like that, just … out there in a world he didn't want me in. I often thought I should talk to him about it, but you know what his shell was like." I moved my head down, then up, once, to show that I knew what he meant, but not that I knew much more. "Then I worked up my nerve one year, and went to see him. Asked him, tried to get him to say what was wrong with me. That was when I realized something was happening to his mind. Game over. Guess I left it too long."

"Wrong with you? Willy there never was anything wrong with you, not where Dad was concerned. I was the one that … I was the one who caused that … whatever happened. That's what's in those papers upstairs. And maybe in this stuff down here."

CHAPTER 17

I was on the sofa-bed in Willy's rec room. A few years ago, I had visited for a weekend, and had to sleep on it, all their kids being home for once. Sofa-beds are an uneasy compromise; as a sofa, this one gave a hint of groaning metal seeking release, even the possibility of becoming an ejection seat; as a bed, it felt like a thin mattress over a lattice of angle irons. The floor was cool, indoor-outdoor carpeting over concrete, and my shoes were upstairs. Willy was reading the manuscript in the living room. I had almost told him that I didn't want Nan to see it, but realized that she would never ask or look, and that Willy knew it was personal between us. I shifted sideways to put my feet up on the sofa, then moved one of the cushions for a backrest. I decided that a new sofa would be a good Christmas present.

The butter box first, as it was first in time, and I hadn't seen it except as something on a shelf for forty-four years. Dad had been interested in those files, and Gramp had gone to some lengths to keep them from him. I remembered the intensity of his purpose that day when he had me bundle the files up.

The top files were all financial, reports from companies Gramp had investments in, a whole pile of information slips from his broker. Then taxes: it was interesting that Gramp, even if you adjusted for inflation, paid very little in taxes. It was a different world then. Below that were three correspondence files, "Family", "Financial", and "Other". I put these aside. There were several files headed "Mine" with names of mines as extensions. I leafed through one labelled "O'Brien" to find a map, several photos of groups of miners with hard hats and carbide lamps, staring at the camera as if wondering what they were doing collectively out in the daylight. Some drilling reports were there with assay results, all signed with a florid "P.Thorpe, Mine Manager". One file was marked "Will", and I could see a succession of wills dating from about 1920 to the final one just months before his death. The signature of that one, laboured and shaky, made with his left hand, was attested to by his lawyer and two witnesses.

I turned to the family correspondence file. He must have decided to start this around 1930. A few letters were from a Harold Thorpe, sent from Hants, England. From the context, he was a half-brother, for there were references to "our" father and to "my" mother and "your" mother, obviously two different women. Harold must have been about ten years younger than Gramp. Gramp's mother had died before his father's remarriage, and the letters centred on the death of my great-grandfather in 1929, and the settling of a small estate. The second letter had a puzzled tone, and the third was definitely aggrieved. Gramp had evidently made some fuss about the estate. The fourth letter just referred to the "enclosed" and said that the writer trusted that there would be no further need to correspond.

Then there was a letter from Evvy, signed "Evelyn" An envelope was attached to it with a straight pin, and the postmark was April 15, 1935, Toronto. The letter was typed, with a faded blue ink signature.

Dear Pa and Ma,

It's hard for me to write this, because I know how unhappy my suddenly leaving home must have made you. I won't go into the reasons for it, except to say that you are not to blame, except maybe that I couldn't expect you to understand some feelings. Now, my reasons seem less important than the fact that I know I have hurt you.

As you can see, I have learned to type, and I was lucky to get a job with a good company. Maybe someday, I'll be able to tell you which company. Don't worry, I have landed on my feet, as they say, and will be all right.

How is Petey? Tell him I miss him and give him a hug for me. Hugs to both of you as well.

I don't want to come home to Haileybury right now. Some things happened that you don't know about, things that hurt me very much, nothing that you could have prevented. But I'm not giving you my address right now. Maybe in another year, I will feel different, but I know that if you could find me, you would try to persuade me to come home or tell you why I ran away, and I can't do either right now. I love you all. Of course I'm using a different name, and even my picture wouldn't be much use to you in finding me.

Your daughter,

Evelyn

Behind this letter was a newspaper clipping, a display ad from the Toronto Telegram of May 2 1935, according to the fading pencilled note on it. It read:

To Evelyn Thorpe:

We received your letter. Please write again. Whatever is the matter can be worked out. We all love you and want you to come home, or at least allow us to come and visit you.

Ma, Pa, and Petey

I put the two pieces of paper side by side. There it was, a family break, sixty years ago. That was right about when Mom and Dad got married in Kirkland Lake. Gramp had used his name in the ad, I guessed, knowing he would want Evvy to come home. I wondered if Dad had ever seen this letter; it wasn't from Vancouver, and I remembered there had been a letter from Vancouver. Evvy was, what, about eighteen when she wrote it, the same age as me when I got hurt in the mine. I tried to picture her. Was I that confident of my feelings at that age?

After that there were some letters from a brother of Nana's, then living in Missouri, and a few from people whose names I didn't recognize, but who were clearly more connected with Nana than with Gramp. Then the second letter from Evvy, the one in 1937. It too had an envelope pinned to it, with the postmark of Vancouver, May 27, 1937. It too was typed:

Dear Ma and Pa and Pete,

It seems heartless of me to be writing to you now, more than two years since the last time. More so, because this is the last letter I will ever write to you.

I saw the ad you put in the Tely. It sort of scared me, because I really meant what I said, that I didn't want to come home or have people in Haileybury know where I was. I can't explain any more than that. That fall, I got a chance at a job out here in Vancouver, and I took it.

Now, I've got to tell you that I'm married, under a name you don't know. All I'm going to tell you about my husband is that he is a good man, kind and gentle to me, and he really loves me. I've told him one big lie, a life story from before he met me. He believes it, and I'm never going to change it. I am happy. I'm twenty now, and we're starting with a whole fresh new life. I think (and this is just a guess right now, but I'm pretty sure) that I'm going to have a baby.

Ma, I know you would like to be a grandmother to my baby. Believe me, I'm going to tell him or her what you are like, that you feel love even though you are far away. Maybe Pete will have children. Did he ever meet a nice girl? It's funny to think there might be cousins growing up not knowing each other. If I could, I'd go back and change some things, but I can't. So I have to say goodbye. Please know that I am happy.

Your loving daughter

I had a wild idea of advertising for someone born in early 1938 of a loving couple in Vancouver, whose mother might or might not have answered to Evelyn or Evvy. Pretty hopeless. And why would such a person want to know that a cousin, a tiring if not aging journalist, was living on the Island?

I slid the letter in under the pile, trying to keep the chronological sequence. The head of the pin caught some paper, and I had to work it free and put the letter in again. Only two letters in this file had envelopes attached, both Evvy's. I guessed Gramp had kept the envelopes to show someone, maybe investigators he'd hired, where the letters had come from. Good, I'm in favour of keeping the documentary evidence straight.

There were a couple more letters from people whose names meant nothing to me. One referred to the start of the war, wondering if Nana shouldn't go home to the safety of the States. Then there was one from Mom.

Her writing was a little different, or maybe my memory had shifted. None of us had good penmanship. And the so-called blue-black ink of those days had a tendency to fade to a light purple-grey. But it was Mom, from the phrasing:

November 12, 1942

Dear Pa,

Thank you for the offer of the house in Cobalt. We will accept it, and as soon as things get sorted out with Pete's allotment, we'll start paying rent, or maybe payments to buy it.

Right now, I have my hands full with young Jimmy and the baby. It's wonderful that you have arranged to have split wood ready, and that someone will be minding the pile. You do know so many people in Cobalt!

Pete is in Newfoundland now. I don't think I am breaking any security rules in telling you that. Are there really German spies on the train from Swastika to Haileybury opening our mail?

Pete is well, misses me (he says) and Jimmy (that I believe!). He can't really miss the baby, little Willy, because the two have never clapped eyes on one another.

Catherine, the two boys are growing like milkweeds. It will be good that we are closer, and you can see them more often. Cobalt is close to Haileybury, even with gas rationing.

Love to you both, Peg

That would have been the house over on Ruby Street, in the Wright Subdivision, the one now vanished. When Dad came back from overseas, he had joined the town police force, replacing a Boer War vet who was retiring from policing at 73, and we had moved into the town-owned house on Nickel Street. A family named Koscinski moved into the Ruby Street house, and, I believe, bought it from Gramp for nine hundred dollars.

The next letter of any interest was a blue folded square of flimsy paper. I remembered these. Soldiers were given these thin sheets of paper with gummed flaps. Folded correctly, they formed their own envelope. Of course the soldier never got to fold them himself; they were passed to a censor, an officer in the unit, who checked them for any details about where a unit was or what they were doing beyond innocuous words like "training". It was from Dad, Cpl. P. Thorpe, Algonquin Regiment, some numbered APO or Army Post Office. It was dated 12 Aug 43. I remembered during the last year of the war, when I was eight or nine, these blue squares would arrive at the post office in bunches. Mom would pick hers up from the postmaster, Major Keeling, a rather irascible old gentleman, but one set apart in Cobalt because he was a genuine VC, a Victoria Cross winner from the Boer War. The letters had to be opened and then sorted by date so that Mom could read them in the order they were written. Even then, a gap-filler might arrive weeks later.

This one was addressed to Gramp. I unfolded it. It was Dad's handwriting, a tight, almost cursive script which had gotten smaller during the war as he tried to fit everything he wanted to say onto an uncompromising square of blue tissue paper. I wondered where all those wartime letters to Mom had wound up — were they still in the other box, in Dad's papers? Mom would have kept them. During the war, each one was opened and handled as if it were a rare manuscript, smoothed out with her hand, and you could see her take a deep breath before starting to read. During the Gulf War a few years ago, there were stories of soldiers communicating, sight and sound, with their families through satellites. In 1943, and more so in 1944 and 1945, the soldier was out there in the blue, the only proof of his continuing existence being these little blue letters, and the lack of definite bad news. In 1944, September, a telegram was delivered to the house from the Defence Department, a new euphemism invented during the war. I those days, the delivery man would wait to see if you were going to reply, or anyway to see your reaction. These telegrams from Ottawa were particularly intriguing to messengers. I remember Mom going pale, and her hands scratching at the envelope, until the messenger took it from her and opened it. It was the only time I ever saw her helpless. The minister regretted to inform her that Sgt. P.H. Thorpe had been wounded and was recuperating in a field hospital in France. You could see Mom flood with relief as she filled in the meaning behind the phrases: "wounded" meant out of action and danger for at least for a time; "recuperating" meant that the wound was not too serious, they would have said something else if he'd lost a limb or his sight; "in a field hospital in France" meant that he had not been evacuated to England as a serious casualty. All of which turned out to be true. In fact, he was back with the regiment in time for the fiasco at the Leopold Canal a few weeks later.

I shook myself. Gram, Mom, Nana, Dad, all dead now. I wondered what right I really had to be picking at the sores. Well, Willy was reading the manuscript upstairs, and the cat was not going to climb back into the bag, or the toothpaste flow back into the tube.

The tightness of the script was unnecessary, for the text took up only a third of the page, and there was none of the flow of narrative I remembered from Mom's readings fifty years before:

> *Dear Ma and Pa,*
>
> *I appreciate what you have done for Peg and the children, regarding the house in Cobalt. The situation in K.Lake wasn't good, even though the rent was controlled. Ma, I know you must be helping in other ways as well. Thank you.*
>
> *Things are going well with me. The war changes a lot of things. When you're an NCO, you have to be thinking two steps ahead a lot. We've really hardened as a battalion now, the officers know what they're doing, the men are in really good shape, and we're ready to take Jerry on any time. I can't tell you where we are right now, but can say I've seen a lot of England, mostly on foot and at night.*
>
> *Pa, when I get back, I want to work harder on locating Evvy. You showed me that letter, but I can't believe that she wants to cut so much away, even though she was awfully unhappy about something before she left. I was too, you know why. One thing this war has taught us is that you don't try to move away from trouble, you face up to it when it starts. I'll be coming back, and I'll be with my family, Peg, Jimmy and Baby Will. Pa, I intend to live where I want, and I will protect my family. You should know that.*
>
> *Your son*
>
> *Pete*

I had expected the hostility because it was a constant in my growing up. Again, I felt that surge of resentment against Dad. Dammit, if he was going to hate his father, why couldn't he at least say why? There was almost a threat in that last paragraph, hands off my family, and the part in the middle, about the regiment, seemed to be saying something about himself, that he wasn't the same person who had left Canada over a year before. I wondered what action he had taken on locating Evvy, and I leafed through the rest of the file quickly. No more flimsy blue squares, nothing more from Dad at all. Maybe he'd written separately to Nana, and she'd kept them herself. Or maybe Gramp had filed selectively, only keeping letters he considered particularly important.

I stood up and stretched. I might be filling in on the feeling tone of the problem, but there was no more light on the facts. The next file was "Correspondence - Financial" It was thick, and I doubted if it had anything in it that I needed to know. I weighed it in my hands.

"How's it going?" Willy had come down the stairs.

"Getting through it. Nothing much I didn't know."

"There was lots in what you wrote that I didn't know. It's going to take a while for me to absorb it. Maybe I'd want to argue some things, too. Did you really see Dad that way?"

"Not totally. I guess when it came to him and his family, yes, he looked that way to me. But there were lots of other times, and he wasn't tight or angry all the time. I loved him, you know that, Willy?"

"I know that. But I'm not too sure an outside reader would. You know, Jim, you're a professional writer, you must know how you've made Jimmy appear."

"Self-centred."

"Worse than that. When it comes to Dad, he's almost destructive, vindictive. You're not like that, Jim, and you never were."

"Maybe you see the best in everybody, Willy. I always thought you were too uncritical." But I knew the opposite was true. As a critic, he had hit on some reticence, some holding back that I, as a writer, could sense but not locate.

"Well, I've got to the point where you had that accident underground. The funny thing is that I can really recognize Mom in the story, but you don't see Dad like I did. About Mom, did she really deck you that night in Huntsville?"

"I said my foot slipped, but I'll never be sure. It was an open hand, but she let me have it full strength, and I probably would have gone down even with both feet set. Some woman! It sure brought that episode to an end."

"I wish she'd let you confront Dad. maybe she was too protective of him. Maybe things could have been worked out then."

I felt absolutely weary. He looked at me, and came over, put his arm around my shoulders. "There's no need to solve everything tonight. Nan's fixing a snack upstairs. Let's tackle it again tomorrow. What you've written is fascinating to me, but I need to let some of it sink in, sleep on it. OK?"

I put the thick file of "Correspondence - Financial" down on the sofa-bed. "That's a good idea. Sleeping, I mean. Willy, I'm sorry to put this load on you, maybe I shouldn't have come."

He didn't answer, just patted me on the shoulder, and we went upstairs.

CHAPTER 18

I woke to find the sun streaming in the window of Willy and Nan's guest room. Until recently, it was Al and Grant's room. Gail was still in the semi-dependency of university, and her room, shared with Robyn as they were growing up, was still known as "Gail's room". Some more snow must have fallen, but the sky was clear now, and the sun had the bright hard clarity of winter in it. On the thirtieth of October, I thought. I could hear movement in the kitchen, and I checked my watch: 8:20. Willy had said they generally went to 9:30 mass at their church, Nativity, and I had startled both by saying I'd like to go with them. Willy had leaned forward, a question pushing him, but subsided with a glance from Nan. I had almost laughed, his curiosity was so palpable. I explained that it was exploratory for me right now, but that I'd been experimenting with church again.

I must have seemed very exploratory at mass. I had, by 1960, virtually given up on religion, before all the changes of the sixties. Also, Vancouver Island is a different diocese, and I had not realized the degrees of variation allowed in the mass in matters of when to stand, when to sit, that people here might kneel while people out west might stand. Anyway, we got through it without me looking too stupid.

I insisted on taking them to brunch, and we chose a roadhouse restaurant on the Schumacher highway, on a hill overlooking Gillies Lake. It was an opulent meal. Nan said, "You and Ken share tastes. He brought us here when he was up in July." Had Ken told me he was going to Timmins? My curiosity must have shown. "Oh, nothing special, some consulting he was doing for the Dome. I think he stayed in the motel next door, cause his hours were going to be strange. He was a bit worried about you, said you hadn't looked up to form when he saw you in the spring. And he didn't want to ask you too directly. You know, both he and Laura miss Dee terribly." I knew what she was saying, but to know and to feel are two different things, and it seemed that my own missing of Dee occupied the universe of feeling, or as much of it as I dared peek at. Then Nan smiled. "You look better to me than his description, more purposeful. I guess Willy is being helpful — he usually is." I knew I had to tell her something of what we were doing.

"I'm trying to sort out something that happened almost forty-five years ago. I think I snarled up something for my Dad, and maybe for the whole family. I could say it's too long ago to matter, or I could say it was all my fault, and that's it, but neither would work. I've got to understand it, and I guess I need Willy as a sounding board." She nodded. "But I don't want to be unfair to you two now. I mean, Willy doesn't have any of the responsibility, so he shouldn't have the trouble."

"Willy would tell you if he thought it was unfair. He tells me."

Willy broke in. "Not too often. It's all right, Jim. It clears some stuff for me, too, or I think it will. Hon, if you don't mind, I'll wait till Jim and I are finished before I give you the details?" Her hand touched his, one of those instant sealings of an agreement. Willy looked at me. "Jim, do you want me to finish the manuscript right now, or do you want to talk about what you've found?"

"Let's go back to your place and talk a bit."

Down in the rec room, I showed him the letters from Evvy and the one from Dad. He held the blue flimsy in his hand. "God, he really did hate him, didn't he?"

"You see the hostility too?"

"Hostility is a mild word. Let me see those Evvy letters again." He looked at them for a long time. "How old was Evvy?"

"Sixteen when she ran away in 1933. Eighteen when she wrote the first letter, twenty when she wrote the second."

"If she wrote them. I doubt she did."

"You mean someone was pretending ... That's pretty cruel, Willy."

"Not as cruel as some other things. Look at it with some detachment, Jim. One summer, a sixteen year old girl runs away from home, from a relatively wealthy home. Her fourteen year old brother is still there, but she doesn't say anything to him. Next year, he leaves. He works underground, he starts a new life, he avoids asking his rich father for anything. Remember what you overheard that day Gramp had his stroke — Dad saying something about Gramp hitting him?"

"You mean Gramp beat Dad?"

"Well, another time you mention Dad telling Mom about a dream, with him about nine, and scared of Gramp. Sounded real to me. I think, yes, Gramp beat Dad, probably over a long time. Then finally, this fourteen, fifteen year old is getting big enough to maybe defend himself, but he's afraid of what might happen if he does, what he himself might do. So he goes."

"Evvy? Do you think Gramp beat her?"

"Maybe. Maybe worse. Evvy's the person in this that no one knows. You mention a picture, a stiff portrait, but I can't even remember that. There's a vacancy there, no one can talk about her, or Dad and Gramp are at each other. Even Mom backed off. Why?" Willy paused, then continued. "I see Gramp differently than you do, Jim. Look, even in your memories, whenever we go there, Nana takes me and Gramp takes you. Did Gramp ever hit you?"

"No. After his stroke, he sometimes looked like he wanted to. But what do you mean, maybe worse? With Evvy."

"Wait a bit on that. Look at Nana first. What's her attitude towards Dad?"

"Approval. Except when he tangles with Gramp."

"And what does he tangle with Gramp about?"

"Evvy, I guess." I could see a bit of what Willy was steering towards.

"Jim, do you buy what I'm saying about Gramp beating Dad?"

"I guess so. Yes, that's pretty clear. I should have seen it before.'

"Hard for you to see at thirteen when you have a huge father and an elderly grandfather. And then you thought you were forced to take sides. So naturally, you wouldn't see Gramp as the aggressor."

"What are you getting at about Nana, Willy?"

"Just that she had to know about Gramp hitting on Dad. I mean, after a kid is five or so, even if spankings were necessary before, they don't work. You know, I had to spank, you probably did too. Right?" I grinned, "But we did it to protect the kid, to get through to him or her, get past that impulsiveness. Not just power. Well, Dad is being beaten at nine, maybe even later, and he runs away at fourteen, fifteen. It was power Gramp was after."

"Do you mean he beat Nana?"

"No, probably not. He had the power over her without that. I wonder what she thought after he had that stroke. But she was conventional, don't you see? Not like Mom. I mean, Nana's friends up in Haileybury, they weren't people she'd ever talk to about her husband and her son. Look at when you decided to go to university. What was her reaction then?"

"Relief. I figured from me."

"Maybe she identified you more with Gramp, but I think the main thing was for her to get out of the house, a house she finally realized she hated."

"That's a bit strong."

"I don't think so. Look how she acted when she talked about Dad and Gramp — as if she couldn't understand Dad's feelings. She'd gotten those years of beatings blocked out of her memory. But what always got to her emotionally?"

"Evvy. That's right."

"And not because Evvy was beaten. If that were it, she would have defended her children, or have blocked it out too. Also, I know kids. If a sixteen year old girl is being beaten, and so is her younger brother, and she decides to run away, she'd take her brother with her. And if she wrote letters back, two, four years later, her tone would have been more like Dad's, defiant, not apologetic. No, Evvy's abuse was worse, it was the kind of thing Nana couldn't come close to acknowledging."

"Sexual? But wait a minute. You said before, IF she wrote those letters."

"In order. Yes, I think it was probably sexual abuse. Look, even in those letters she was supposed to have written, there's this hint of something shameful. Something a very clever, very power hungry, abuser would put in."

"And Nana knew?"

"Probably not on the same level she knew Dad was being beaten. I mean, there were probably lots of plausible reasons for the beatings, and Nana was cowed enough to accept them. Then, with Dad grown up and OK, she can feel all right because look, he survived, maybe it did him some good like Gramp probably claimed. But her daughter being a sex object of her husband, no, that's too painful to think about. And her daughter disappears. Does she know the reason? In a way she does, but every time she thinks of Evvy, she's just dipping into a well of pain so concentrated that rationality doesn't enter into it."

"You said 'disappears', not 'runs away'."

"You've got to know by now, Jim, that the body you found in the mine was probably Evvy. I mean you've been writing circles around that point. That was Dad's suspicion, that's what you were frustrating him in."

"Not deliberately, I swear, Willy."

"Oh no, it was one of those incremental things, what a tangled web we weave, et cetera. But you were protective of Gramp, and you did take sides. And I'm pretty sure you know what Evvy's birthstone was."

"Amethyst." He was right, I had looked it up. Sometime after I found out her birth month. "But that would mean that Gramp…"

"Murdered her. It doesn't shock me as much as it does you. I mean you've seen just about every kind of atrocity in this world, but I doubt if you've ever known an abuser, known someone for years as a parent of a kid you've taught, avoided thinking about it when you see that something is going terribly wrong with the child. Then when it comes out, why the abuser is so injured! So betrayed! Someone has challenged the secret power, and it's so unfair! By that time, the kid has been used in such a way, that the powerful one just sees her as an object. I've seen parents who would happily kill the child if that would make the old power come back, and the respect and the reputation. And I've seen wives stick by these bastards."

"Did Dad know this?"

"Oh, I doubt it very much. Less than Nana. But his sister disappeared, and he probably loved her more than anyone else in the world. I mean, how could he trust Nana — she must have seemed complicit in what was happening to him. He probably didn't know what was happening to Evvy because she wouldn't tell anyone. Just rebelled against the abuser one night, a sixteen year old who took on the dragon and was beaten to death. Was that courage or desperation?' Maybe both, we don't know Evvy. Then he dragged her into an old stope, already ice forming under a drip. He beat her face in down there, probably. Maybe didn't even see the ring."

I could see Gramp's face, hear him call out "Jimbo!". I believed Willy in a way, but still there was that face. Did he make me a favourite to show Dad power? Why had he given that house to Mom during the war? I felt as if I were looking at one of those optical illusions, the ones with all the colours in a jumble on the page, and then when you focus <u>past</u> the page, if you're lucky, a three dimensional image forms. Now I was seeing Gramp, a young son named Pete, a pretty daughter, a scared wife. The image jumped out at me of that stope underground, the ice, the arm, but sticking out of the ice, the glint of the amethyst in the light of the carbide lamp. A blink of an eyes, and I saw Gramp in a hospital bed, a tall policeman standing at the foot of the bed. Nemesis.

"Willy?"

"Here."

"I think I have to take a break. I mean this may be obvious to you, but it's startling to me."

"Well, you journalists are kind of protected. I'm a teacher. Sorry, Jim. I know it's rough. But your manuscript, you know, shows that you were sort of moulding the evidence, and every time you hit something inconvenient or frustrating, why, there was Dad, the cause of it all. If I'd hit the same conflict of loyalties at thirteen, fourteen, I'd probably have made the same mistake. But I wasn't and I didn't."

And wouldn't have. I think I referred to Willy before as sweet-natured — had he read that part? and had he blushed? — but I'd just had a taste of tough-mindedness. His sweetness didn't come from naivety, just from fairness after clear assessment. "I'll just sit here for a while, OK?"

"Sure. Look, I've <u>got</u> to get some of those projects marked before tomorrow. It's almost four, and Nan has something planned for six. See you then." And he went up the stairs. The smarter brother. I think I'll call him Mycroft from now on.

I looked at my new world view with some curiosity. Nana. She'd sold that house like a shot. We'd seen her for one Christmas a few years later. Then the winters in Florida lengthened, she gave up the Toronto apartment, and the next we knew, she was in Arizona. Christmas cards, nice monetary gifts on birthdays. I saw her once in Tucson, 1970 or so, and introduced Dee to her. She died in 1973, almost eighty, and that was the end of her. Dad flew down, I understood, but there was nothing there. She'd pared her life down to a few card-playing friends, a condo with leased furniture, and a will leaving her effects and belongings to a charity in Arizona. Canada, Cobalt, Haileybury, a family, all might have been as a dream to her. It fit with what Willy had said.

I was thinking that the boy genius Jimmy Thorpe had been remarkably dense for a number of years, maybe forty-five. Sexual and physical abuse, right in my own family, and there I had gone, participating in a cover-up. IF it was true, a nagging little defensive voice said. Gramp had been gruff, maybe a bit of a bully, liked to have his way and got it, but that didn't add up to the monster Willy had described. Could it be that teaching today had become so rough that it turned practitioners into cynics?

Picking up the next file was not a search for corroborating or exculpatory material. It was more to have something to do with my hands and my eyes. "Correspondence- Financial" would be dull and that was what I wanted. If my journalist self were alive, the file might have suggested a series on robber barons in Canadian mining in the twenties and thirties. All it told me now was that Gramp was smart and ruthless, financially. Not that he was or was not a murderer.

"Correspondence - Other" was a total hodgepodge, no order except chronological. I combed through 1933 from late spring to fall with no result. I hardly expected him to say anything, but I thought he might have written to someone about his daughter running away, and that the tone might tell me something.. But the copies of his outgoing correspondence did not mention his loss, nor did the flow of correspondence slow. 1935 gave the same picture. I was thinking 1937 would too, when I was caught by a letter from Vancouver. The date was May 29, 1937. Maybe Gramp would have seen the postmark and thought Evvy had changed her mind. I could see him tearing it open, calling to Nana.

It turned out to be a long and wordy letter from a Harry Farley, a mining consultant (engineering, not geology). It was gossipy, opening with a series of references to mining people in BC who had worked in Cobalt at one time or another, mutual acquaintances. Then there was a discussion of mining activity in the Similkameen Valley, a Mascot Mine and the particular challenges it presented, challenges earning Farley good money at the time. Then a short paragraph, the second last in a long three page letter:

I did what you wanted and popped that envelope into the mail at the main post office the other day. Didn't even steam it open to find out what you were up tom, mailing letters to yourself. Some scheme to reassure a nervous investor, I'll bet. You'll never change, Pete.

There it was, proof that the second letter from Evvy was faked. And that made the first letter a fake as well. No wonder Gramp hadn't wanted Dad to get his hands on these files. Even a simple analysis would show the two Evvy letters to be typed on the same machine, probably right in the study in Haileybury. It was one thing to show that second Evvy letter to a young private soldier going overseas. It was quite another to have a police officer, one with suspicions high, examining it. I wondered at Gramp keeping this letter from Farley. Arrogance, young Pete married and in the army, Catherine submissive, what could there be to worry about. Or maybe he wanted to follow up on something else Farley wrote, kept the letter for a while, and simply forgot.

I put down the file, keeping Farley's letter out, and went up the stairs. Willy was at the coffee table, trying to sort out the components of a student project. I put the letter on top, and watched as he read it. He jabbed his finger at the paragraph.

I spoke first. "You told me so."

"Are you sad?"

"In a way, I guess. I loved him, you know. And when he had that stroke, it seemed unfair. But hubris got him, didn't it?"

Willy folded the letter. "Is this the end of it, Jim?'

"I don't know. I'm still going to look through Dad's stuff. Maybe there was something else, besides me, throwing him off. Like maybe it wasn't ALL my fault. But not tonight. Let's drop it for a while — I'm not really ready to talk about it."

It was Nan who kept the conversation up during dinner, comparing the vicissitudes of the BC and Ontario NDP governments. I think she is a socialist of the old Tommy Douglas school, which made her comments searing. I didn't have the energy to pontificate, probably the easiest mode of discussion. After dishes, I excused myself for a walk. Willy was only half way through the projects.

I almost got lost in the maze of streets, crescents and dead-ends. Then I saw traffic whipping past at speeds that indicated the highway. When I worked over to it, I was right beside that pub, and I was chilled. Something hot, or if they had a fireplace going, a beer.

Fred Guest was at the same place he'd been yesterday, elbows going out impossibly far, smoke curling up, a beer in front of him. He might have been posing for a Toby jug, and as if I had said something out loud, he turned, saw me, and grinned at me. There was nothing to do but join him.

Then there was nothing to do but accept the beer he offered me. "Those print-outs work out OK?" Nod on cue. "How long you staying with Willy?"

Maybe a week? I thought this, and said it. He nodded judiciously, as if he'd considered the matter and thought a week should do the trick. "Willy talks a lot about you. Looks up to you, I'd say."

Fat lot you know. But he went on. "Says that you stick with a story till it's really done, not just off to the next high spot. Said you might be the one to do a Watergate on Mulroney, but you retired before anyone assigned you to it." I murmured something, getting more uncomfortable. "Tell me, Jim … it is Jim isn't it? Tell me, how do you <u>know</u> when a story's done. I mean there's always loose ends, aren't there?"

I wondered how drunk he was. Probably about the same as yesterday. I used to know a guy on the *Star* in Toronto who was like that. "On maintenance" was how he described it, enough alcohol in him that whatever pain was working on him was dulled, and yet his brain found a way to compensate. Never at top pitch, but never incoherent. I forget what I told Fred Guest, or how I got away, but the bit about loose ends stuck with me all the way back to Willy's house. In this story, I was a loose end, maybe Willy was too, no matter how neatly woven his life appeared, maybe Laura and Ken were too.

When you're a loose end of some fabric, do you just accept it and wait for the last of those three Fates, the one with the shears? Or do you seek a pattern you and the other loose ends can cooperate in making? Me Warp, you Woof, let's weave it. God, I was tired.

CHAPTER 19

Nan and Willy were both gone when I woke on Monday. Nan was working as a teacher aide, taking a boy with severe cerebral palsy through the day. She had left a note in the kitchen telling me where to find things in the fridge.

I'm glad she didn't come home at lunch to see what I'd done to her kitchen. I used the table and every inch of counter space to sort the contents of the box of Dad's papers. I decided to use chronology for the first sort. Then, of course, I hit my first snag. What was I looking for?

If it was just the investigation of the body in the mine, I could start with 1949 and end with 1950. Relations with Gramp? Start as early as possible, go to 1952, maybe a few years later, until Nana effectively left our lives. With the bulging box at my feet, and only a few items out on the counters, I decided that I simply didn't know what I was looking for, and I'd just work through the lot, hoping that something would jump out and bite me.

One thing did, quickly. There was an undated envelope, filled with something — crumpled paper? I opened it, and slid out some tissue. I knew what it was before unfolding the tissue. The amethyst ring. From the mine, from the hand in our shed, from its hiding places, even from the grave, here it was, evidence. But not evidence a policeman deposited in some evidence locker. No, he'd kept it, a puzzle about where it came from, a symbol of a split between him and his son, a memento of a lost beloved sister. Not official.

In the piles of material, there was nothing before 1945, and only one item from that year, a canvas covered Army Field Notebook. It was a diary he'd kept in Germany from the end of hostilities in May through the summer and early fall as the unit dwindled. Some departed for Canada early, having volunteered to continue active service in the Far East, the war against Japan. For them, it was a gamble that paid off: Dad's first reaction to the news of the atomic bomb and Japan's surrender was relief that some of his friends wouldn't be in a continuing war, mixed with a little envy that they were back with their families. There were lots of references to us. Mom's letters were noted with little "PEG"s and dates, and our progress in photos were commented on. His service points were good, so his turn came in early September. He described his arrival in Cobalt a few days after the event, but I was already seeing it as a nine year old, the rushing black locomotive, the clouds of steam, the huge drive wheels, the screech of air brakes. A silver band was playing — yes, there were Welsh in Cobalt — "When Johnny Comes Marching Home", and an impossibly huge man was scooping me up and hugging me, his cheek rough, his kitbag strap sliding down to his elbow on an arm that didn't seem to notice the weight any more than if it were a small purse. Willy, sensibly, had taken refuge behind Mom's skirt, and she was turning, laughing, to grab him and lift him for inspection.

The whole diary was empty of any mention of Gramp. Nana yes, how she cooked a celebratory dinner. He discussed the pros and cons of becoming a policeman when he was offered the job. Old Bill Wykeham, 73 and a veteran of the Boer War plus the Great War, was admitting his inability to handle the younger roughs, and was throwing in the towel. The money was pretty poor, but not bad, compared to a sergeant's pay. It was the town-owned house that made the deal, after Dad saw what we were living in on Ruby Street. The one on Nickel Street was big enough, had a furnace with hot aid ducts to the whole main floor, a furnace that could burn wood or coal. It was a substantial place that would have rented for thirty-five dollars a month. Nothing to sneeze at.

In the 1946 pile, there were some photographs of the big victory parade in North Bay, when the last of the regiment came home at the end of January. In the spring, our whole family went to Toronto for Dad's award of the Military Medal. Gramp had arranged for two compartments on the train, and Dad had choked back his objections for once. Those are the two things I remember: the hugeness of Convocation Hall at the University, so big that Dad and the small man pinning the medal to his chest (The Governor-General, Alexander of Tunis, but if the King had been in Canada, I told my friends, he would have done it) were doll-like figures there in the centre of the sphere; the other thing was that it was the first time I noticed the anger and dislike between Dad and Gramp.

In the spring of 1947, I found the letter from my teacher, telling Dad that I should write the High School Entrance exams, though I was still in Grade Seven. She said that I "needed more challenge", which might just have indicated her desire to get a little know-it-all moved along. Also in 1947, Dad started keeping additional journals, supplementary to his official police reports. The official papers would be in the police files, now with the OPP. These notes were sparse, often not complete sentences, names mostly, for example, "Geo. Hadley 65 Galena, domestic. Warned" or "Jack Kelley, no fixed address, slept in cell>' The first years were in scribblers with a big 5 on the cover, and a hundred pages of grey newsprint. The pencil notes were hard to read. I would find in later piles that he switched to better paper and a fountain pen.

At three-fifteen, I woke to the mess around me. I found a big box of rubber bands, and began bundling the year-piles back into the box I had all week, and Nan wouldn't want her kitchen looking like an archival workroom. Her charge would be picked up by a HandiBus promptly, leaving her free for an errand or two before she picked Willy up at his school, provided he wasn't coaching something. They arrived together, just after four. Nan was carrying a bag which turned out to be mostly candy, and Willy had two big shopping bags filled with those little packets of potato chips. Of course, it was Hallowe'en. After a short and early supper, we took turns at the door, doling out stuff to a succession of witches, cats, rabbits, clowns, princesses, cowboys, lizards from Jurassic Park, lions from Central Africa, and a host of Disney characters. Later the streams thinned, than came in driblets, until our sole customers were teenagers who thought a dark raincoat and a scowl was sufficient disguise.

Before the eleven o'clock news, Willy and I sat with cups of herbal tea. "Haven't got back to your manuscript yet. Tomorrow." he said.

"I'm not even sure the rest is necessary. No, it must be, I mean the Gramp thing isn't the whole story, is it?"

"Nothing's ever the whole story. There's always loose ends. Depends on how far you want to follow things."

His remark about loose ends reminded me. "I ran into Fred Guest last night, on my walk."

"In the pub. Would have to be. That's Fred's office. What do you think of him?

"Is he drunk in school?"

"No. Hungover, always. Funny, do you remember the set of novels by Robertson Davies? The central character, the narrator, in the first book is Dunstan Ramsay. He talks about teaching in a private boys' school, says that the private school is the last refuge of the eccentric teacher, the type that can't survive in the public system. Ramsay says that those are the memorable teachers in a kid's life, often for the good. Fred's like that. He's a real headache to administrators, late with everything, chaotic in his record-keeping, even kind of dispiriting to see coming through the door, late more often than not. His clothes usually look like he's slept in them, and I think he often has. Altogether, a deplorable example to the kids. But the kids love him."

"Just because he's anarchic?"

"No, more because he follows the first bit of the real teacher's code, the same as the doctor's: first, do no harm. He likes kids, listens to them, knows their names, their friends. There's some other teachers in our system who have neat rooms, beautiful bulletin boards, lesson plans to a T, perfect records of attendance, test marks, everything like that, and they are kid destroyers. They don't like them. They enjoy power, even the fake power of 'school discipline'. Damn few administrators see through them. Fortunately, most administrators see Fred as a necessary evil, their personal cross to bear, and he survives. Not forever. Eventually one of those power freaks will be principal, and that'll be it for Fred."

I don't dream often, or I should say they don't stay with me often. It might have been the atmosphere of Hallowe'en, but the nightmare I had, the one that woke me at three AM was a doozy. I was hurrying through impossibly narrow streets, cobblestones, rough walls jutting out on both sides to form a jumble of angles. I was chasing someone. Every so often, light coming from around the next corner would throw the shadow of my quarry on a wall, and I would rush ahead only to find that he or she had gotten around the next corner. Eventually, the shadows became clearer in outline. He had a rounded head, and was stooped, with short legs, even though the light made them elongated in the shadows on the walls. He was carrying something, no, someone, a girl whose hair streamed down. The streets were going downhill, and the walls were streaked with moisture There was no rain, no light from above, only a glow ahead, with whatever gave off the light retreating before the man and his burden. I speeded up, to no avail.

I was stopped by a huge hand on my shoulder. My first thought was that Dad was after me, and I tried to shake free, Then I looked at the hand, long fingers, nicotine stained, not Dad's. It was Fred Guest.

There was no sound in my dream. His mouth moved, but I could hear nothing. He shook his head. Worried that my quarry was getting away, I looked down the narrow street for the light. It had disappeared. I could see the street winding down, farther than I could see before, drawn in blocks of blue-grey like the backgrounds of an animated film, but no shadow of the man and his burden. Fred shook my shoulder impatiently. I looked back at him and saw that his other arm, cigarette in hand, was pointing back up the street. There was another light up there somewhere, and a different shadow that coalesced into the shadow of a large man, erect, not stooped like Fred. Beside him were two other shadows, two children, his shadow hands resting on their shoulders, not possession but protection. Two boys? The taller one might have been a girl.

I knew I'd been running down these streets for a long time, and I was tired as I climbed back up them. As I knew it would, the shadow receded. I looked back for Fred, but he was gone. Just the smell of his cigarette. Then I woke up.

There was no question in my mind that the man I'd been chasing was Gramp, and the girl he was carrying was Evvy. Or that the shadow up higher was Dad. What I resented in a way was this oracular figure, this Fred Guest, telling me to stop chasing one and try to get to the other. I thought I was already doing that.

I went to the kitchen to get a glass of milk. I went back to the feeling tone of the dream, and realized that the chase, the attempt to catch the man wasn't in anger or to stop him, but to try to get him to turn and greet me, show that he was doing nothing wrong, to love me.   Get Gramp to call me "Jimbo" one more time. That's why I had been stopped. There was no love to be gotten there. Murderers don't love; they have written themselves out of humanity, they are riding an axis of power and fear, and all they have is self-regard. Shakespeare has Claudius talk about the primal curse, a broth-er's murder. Where does the murder of a daughter lie on that scale? And what was I to Gramp but a decoy, or maybe a shield against the nemesis of her brother, his son?" I thought back to that year when I lived in the house, before Gramp died, when I helped take care of him. I had often felt his rage, and always thought it was directed at the stroke, his disability. But no, he had hated Nana and me because we were alive and well, and we had not shielded him from this and from his son.

As I went back to bed, I wondered if this was going to be one of those two-parters, a serial dream. It wasn't. I woke in time to share breakfast with Willy and Nan. Tonight I would do the cooking, I told them. No, I'd get the groceries on my walk, I'd seen the grocery beside the little plaza with the pub.

In a way, the dream speeded me up, gave me a clue to what I was looking for. I stopped combing everything for traces or echoes of Gloria Peet or Evelyn Thorpe. Dad, whatever his suspicions, had no hard facts to work on. Instead, I was looking for Dad himself, how he thought, what he felt.

In July of 1949, he recorded my return from Ipperwash Cadet Camp: "Jimmy came back on the train last night, all full of soldier pride. Pray God he never has to find out what soldiers really do. He's still so small, I feel he's helpless, but he is thirteen, sharp, trying to grow up." The next month: "Jimmy and young Harry found a body in the old Gibson Mine. They'd been cutting ice down there, an old stope, terribly dangerous. Should be keeping a closer eye. Body of a girl, mid teens, down there over ten years I bet. I thought of Evvy. Got to be careful."

And then: "Pa had stroke last night. I may have caused it, had fight about Evvy's letters. Didn't mean to, didn't really want to make him pay. He's a cruel man, but that's him. Ma is mad at me. I'm sorry for her, or am I? She hasn't been herself for a long time, only looks happy when Peg is with her. Thank God for Peg." Later in the same notebook: "Last day on the job, over to Jim and a young OPP coming in next week. I think I'll miss a lot of it, sort of like soldiering , without the killing, cleaner. Off to KL with Wright-Hargreaves, Security. Company cop. Better money, tho, and kids away from Pa."

There was no diary for our year in Kirkland lake, and then, with the OPP, he started them again., back to the laconic entries. No mention of the amethyst ring., Worry about Willy having to change schools, and my weekend visits were mentioned. Once particularly: "Peg tells me Jimmy came up last night while I was doing double shift, and she sent him away. She says he was spoiling for a fight about the ad for Evvy. ???? Sometimes I don't understand the kid. Seventeen now."

In 1954, he showed approval of me getting out of the mine and into university. "J. is going to Western now. I was worried about him stalling, staying underground. Hard to talk to him still. Things should get better. Ma in Toronto, seems a different person." He liked me taking COTC and going to the School of Infantry in Camp Borden. "This will be good for Jim. He needs confidence (not cockiness). They'll push him a bit there, but he'll be OK."

1956 had three notebooks. The first started Jan 1, the second in April, and the third in August. A quick leaf through showed nothing but work-related stuff in the first. I feared I knew what would be in the second, and I was right. Three pages in, and I found it. There was a short note on mileage and shift times for the day before Mom's death. Then a blank page, and an outpouring began three days after her funeral, Monday morning, obviously an hour or two after I had piled into the old Plymouth, leaving him and Willy in North Bay.

They've put my poor Peggy in the ground. There will never be another like her. Twenty-two years ago, we met, me a busboy, and her a sharp-tongued pretty young waitress. You didn't want to on the wrong side of her! It started that she was fun to be with, and then I needed to be with her, for she could almost read my mind. and even then she liked me. I was full in love by the time the resort closed in September, and I hitched up to Kirkland Lake to look for a job.

I got down to Toronto when I could. Her house was nice on the outside, but her father — well, he didn't like me, and he sure had a rough side for Peg. I'll never know why she decided to love me. She was never the falling kind, I'm sure she looked me over and thought a bit. I guess my need for her showed like a signal fire.

She died of an aneurism in the brain, a time bomb the doctor called it, the weakness being there from birth and no one could tell when it would let go. She had a headache, and two hours later she was gone. I can still hardly take it in. Willy can't. The poor boy is just walking in a fog. I don't know if I can ever fill in the huge gaping hole torn in his life. I can't, in fact, and there's a reason I shouldn't try.

Jim came home right away from London, and for a while seemed to be completely grown up, taking care of the two of us, me being about as useful as a chunk of wet paper. I say "seemed" because he couldn't keep it up. I saw it overseas how many times, the kid in the platoon who you swore would never do more than piss his pants, suddenly faces a tight thing and becomes a man, does things you thought he never could, and there you're thinking there's good NCO material out of nothing, and then ... it's just too much for him and he's back to where he was, maybe worse.

Anyway, Jim did help us, getting us up to Cobalt, sort of running that house we borrowed, right through the funeral. Then the pressure was off, and he just disappeared on us — went up to Haileybury and got soaked. I can't complain at that, I was doing the same thing in Cobalt, once Willy went to sleep. I heard him crying in there, looked in, and saw that he was sound asleep, just sobbing. It broke me up, and I reached for a bottle.

Jim came in about 1:30. I could tell he was drunk, and maybe I was too, and I guess I expected him to be like Willy, to let loose with his sorrow — it had to be there. I said something, something stupid probably, about letting it out. He seemed to get enraged, and he started in on me, calling me names. I was holding his shoulders, and his arms were sort of flailing, not coming near me he was so out of it. Then he started shouting, and I told him to shush because Willy was sleeping. I don't think he heard me. He stared at me and shouted louder, then I heard what he was saying. "What did you do to her, why, why, I know you gave poor Gramp that stroke, what did you do to Mom, why did she have to have a stroke too?" That much was clear, but there was more, hateful garbage, about Evvy and how I thought more of her than of Peg, and I couldn't stand it.

I hit him. A short right, and I remember the feel of my fist on the side of his head, Spit flew out of his mouth. His arms were down, shaking at his side. I hit him again, and drew back for the third punch. He would have been sliding down, but my left hand had a grip on his shoulder. He was still light, I could have held him off the ground at arm's length. As my fist went forward the third time, I thought, I was surprised to think, "This is good!" I was enjoying it. I had never thought to feel joy again with Peg gone, and here it was, so simple! My fist landed, and he slumped completely. I carried him with my left hand grip on his shoulder, and let him slide onto the sofa he'd been sleeping on for three nights. Then I went to the bathroom and got sick.

I had only one clear thought. If I was going to start beating up my kids, even one twenty years old and inviting it like hell, and particularly if it was going to be fun for me, then I couldn't see a helluva lot of difference between me and Pa. And if there was no difference, what was going to happen to me and to my family? Was Peg the only thing that kept me sane?

I had to break this thing, this streak in our family, right off, right now.

I washed Jim's face. The bleeding from his cheek was already clotting. He'd be sore in the morning. I sat there a while, then wrote a note to him. I spent the next few hours walking, all the places Peg and I knew in Cobalt. I slid into the house after dawn, changed, ate a bit, then went over to the church. I wouldn't be able to go to communion with food in my belly, and certainly not with my right fist skinned.

I knew, there in church, what I'd have to do. Not what the Church would suggest, not by a long shot, but they didn't know Pa, and Pa's blood runs in my veins. Damn it. I saw a guy over there who suddenly realized he liked war, or the excitement of shooting and, maybe, killing someone. He did the most sensible thing. He just shut down the emotions, just made himself stay calm, cool, collected, became a technician. I've got to do something like that. I cannot, will not, _feel_ about the boys. Feeling is just too easy to flip, good for bad, love for hate, need for someone for power over that someone.

So, this morning, I went through the show of forgiving Jim and asking him to forgive me. It was a show, because I will never forget what he said about Peg, and I will never forgive myself the feeling I had while hitting him. I think I can handle it, this pulling away from the boys. It will be harder with Willy, because I know he would never give me a plausible reason for hitting him. And it's him I'll be with more. But I know this blood now, I know an excuse would come along if I felt hard enough, so I'll cut the feeling, turn down the volume. I can do it, I know I can, because I have to. The way I felt about Peg, I can't afford to be that strong in feeling ever again.

Jim shouted something about Evvy at me, saying it was an obsession with me. That's something else I have to shut down. She's dead, I know that in my heart, I've known it for a long time. Pa is dead too. Let the dead bury the dead. Jim is alive, Willy is alive. Peg is dead, and she's the one I owe so much to.

There were two blank pages after that, as if he thought he might come back and add something. He didn't. The rest of the booklet was taken up with the terse notations of highway patrol out of North Bay.

I kept the booklet to myself that night, wondering whether to show it to Willy, to admit that I was the cause, some drunken outburst. Then I thought that if I started up a new cycle of hiding things, it would be a betrayal of Dad, all over again.

So, Wednesday, after he came home, I gave him the booklet and went for a walk. I didn't go near the pub. I didn't need or want any more of Fred Guest's advice. I went south along the river, finding a road that wound behind the big white high school on the ridge. Nan, I knew, was out at a dinner meeting. I gave Willy two hours, then went back.

I could see he'd been crying. "He was a brave man, wasn't he, Jim?"

"None braver. He did that just after losing Mom. Willy, I feel like a first class bastard."

"You didn't do anything thousands of kids haven't done. I think he just looked his father in the face and defeated him. You know, even when I was a kid, I wondered how, with what happened, how he managed that … control. I thought Mom was the answer, and she was, in a way, but after, well, he did it himself, didn't he? I mean choked off something evil. That last paragraph, do you think he realized Gramp killed Evvy? Or thought so?"

"I don't know," And I didn't. I thought about the last years of his life, and wondered if the Alzheimers had been a washing out of pain in some ways. I didn't know that either.

CHAPTER 20

The plane's acceleration pushed me back in my seat, then the tilt came, that sharp turn out of Toronto International Airport. We'd be in Edmonton in five hours. I set my watch back two hours, right here, with the plane still climbing. Laura had sounded puzzled that I was visiting. She'll have to get used to the idea that I love her and that I intend to see more of her. And Ken, of course. If Dad had shut down feeling to protect us, I owed it to him to stop my shutting down, because mine was just self-indulgence.

I had a good visit with Ken, who hadn't even known I was in the East before I showed up on his doorstep. I didn't show him this manuscript. Willy and I had agreed that it was pretty well between us. "And Nan," I amended. Dee would have had a right to know as well. But the next generation was far enough away from Haileybury and Cobalt in the thirties and forties. It's not one of those cute family stories you include in the albums. It may have emotional resonance for Willy and me, but not for them. It's up to me and Willy, especially me, to honour Dad. And Evvy, the unknown victim. Is it slighting her to keep her secret, do we run the danger of hiding both her and Gramp, and somehow equating them? I hope not, and think not, for I have a feeling that I can recover prayer. Anyway, we owe the debt to the man we knew and the sacrifice he made. Let the dead bury the dead.

I stayed until November seventh with Willy and Nan, then went to the TriTown for a few days. Willy carted the stone down on the following Saturday. By that time, I'd gotten permission from the parish priest, a thin young man named Bracken, successor to a long line of squarish florid Irishmen. I had explained that my brother and I had recently established to our own satisfaction that an aunt was dead, though there had been some doubt. We wanted to place a small stone in the cemetery, near our parents' stones. Not a question of interment, not a marker, just a memorial.

"No disturbance of the grounds?"

"Just spading a small place to set the stone. It will be flush, like my father's." I had gone to look. When Dad died, his ashes went beside Mom's grave, and Willy had placed a flush stone beside the upright one marking Mom's place.

"Are there ashes?"

There were, in a way, but I hadn't intended to let the priest know. "Yes, we want to scatter them. There's not much."

"Was there a service?" Yes, Father, enough services. Evelyn Thorpe, buried as Gloria Peet forty five years ago, Mr. Peter Thorpe, well known mining executive and secret monster. Peggy Thorpe, source of sanity, Sergeant Peter Thorpe, upholder of public order, cleanser. Catherine Thorpe, down in Arizona, finally escaped from the horror by denial, withdrawal, death.

"Yes," The ashes were in a brown paper bag in a drawer in my motel room in Haileybury. Willy and I had conducted the service over his barbecue in the back yard, whisking the snow off it first. Files from

Gramp's desk, kept for years in a wooden butter box, flamed along with some notebooks filled with the tight cursive script of our father's.

So, on the Saturday, we want in Willy's car to that cemetery. The ground was frozen, but we chipped away at it with a short D handled spade and dug out the few inches necessary. The stone was small, but heavy, when we got it from the trunk. First I placed a small envelope containing an amethyst ring in the centre of the hole, then the stone. Willy patted dirt back along the edges:

IN MEMORY OF
EVELYN THORPE
1917 - 1933

I showed Willy the gravestone marked "Gloria Peet". It had been a thin slab of limestone, and the weathering had almost obliterated the letters. We said a prayer there, then went back to Mom and Dad and said another. The ashes we just strewed around and the wind took them.

Willy was heading right back, and he dropped me at the motel. We'd said our goodbyes, and I'd extracted a promise of a nice long visit to the Island next summer. He reminded me of my promise to visit Ken and Laura. I was not going to forget. Already, I had a resolve about my family, and I knew it would take deeds, action, expression, before the aura of another me would harden and take shape. But not the opacity of all those Russian dolls. Too much theory, too much metaphor. Be more of a father, and maybe you'll get to be an involved grandfather, and a good one.

The plane climbed above the clouds, and the grey wisps transformed into brilliance below us.